I0682539

SAY
NO TO
HEARTBREAKS

SUBHASH CHANDRA BOSE

First published in 2017 by

Becomeshakespeare.com
Wordit Content Design & Editing Services Pvt Ltd
Unit - 26, Building A-1, Nr Wadala RTO, Wadala (East),
Mumbai 400037, India
T:+91 8080226699

WORDIT ART FUND

This book has been funded by the Wordit Art Fund. Wordit Art Fund
helps deserving authors publish their work by providing monetary
support. To apply for funding, please visit us at
www.BecomeShakespeare.com

Copyright © 2017 by Subhash Chandra Bose
All rights reserved. Any unauthorized reprint or use of this
material is prohibited. No part of this book may be reproduced or
transmitted in any form or by any means, electronic or mechanical,
including photocopying, recording, or by any information storage
and retrieval system without express written permission from the
author/publisher.
Please do not participate in or encourage piracy of copyrighted
materials in violation of the author's rights. Purchase only
authorized editions.

©
ISBN: 978-93-86487-70-4

DEDICATION

Dedicated to my mom, who inspires me towards being better every day, all my friends who believed in me and my readers who made my writing spree fantasy, real.

ACKNOWLEDGMENTS

I thank everyone who supported me with writing this book
all along. Especially my friends who took their time in
reading the script to give some very important suggestions.
I thank Malini Nair who came up with the proposal for my
book and believing in it. I thank Sri Charan for his
photography that gave me a beautiful cover.

PREFACE

If you haven't been in pain, you've never been in love. We all have a story that can't be told; a story that defines us and what we've become; a story that could either kill us, or help us push ourselves; a story which no one else but us, can fathom.

There are more heartbreaking stories than happily ever after ones. The grieving later turns into dealing with reality, with a smile. We start pretending, as we accept life the way it is.

I ran into an old friend from college at the coffee shop one summer evening.

"Long time. How are you doing?" I asked, as he gave me a hug getting up his chair.

"Life goes on." He said, with a smile.

It felt weird. It wasn't the guy I knew back in college. He was sweet, fun and made friends like, in a click. He had a perfect life. "Waiting for someone?" I asked, as I had to go in and join my friends.

"Nah." He said pulling out a pack of cigarettes and a lighter. "I just come here once in a while to have coffee."

"Everything ok?" I asked him suspiciously. Because back then, we considered smoking as a sin and I was surprised to see a friend who was almost the most perfect guy, puff out a cloud of smoke.

"Everything's perfect." He lied through his teeth. I couldn't probe him further. I only met him after two years and I didn't want to be meddlesome.

"How's your girlfriend?" I asked.

"You remember?" he chuckled.

"Duh? You were the only one in college with a high school sweetheart. You guys were together for seven years and it was great. Not many last that long." I went on.

"She got married a year ago." He smiled, looking straight into my eyes, sipping his coffee. I shot him a blank stare. There was no regret in his eyes. He felt fine. His smile seemed bright, as if he only just fell in love.

"I'm sorry." I apologized. "What happened?"

"Nah. We just didn't outthink how to convince our families." He continued smiling. I couldn't say another word. So we caught up for the past two years and I asked if he was seeing someone else again. "I've been in few other relationships for the last two years since we broke up, but didn't go well. Same old same old. The next girl, I was in a hurry. I thought she could distract me from my past and I could move on which later turned out to be a disaster. Apparently she was only attracted to me and wasn't serious." He sarcastically spoke, without losing his smile. "The next girl said she was deeply in love with me but I was merely a pit stop."

"What does that mean?"

"Well, she was all like 'you're my life' kind of a girl until her ex boyfriend came back and she started saying she still had feelings for him. It didn't pan out."

"Crazy, dude." I gasped. "We never thought something like this would happen to you."

"That's life, my friend. We never know what's in store for us." He smiled. He just smiled.

"So what now?" I asked.

"My parents found a girl. She's good; sweet. She knows my darkness. Talks are going on. Let's see what happens."

"Sure about that?"

"Of course not. Life goes on, man. If we start accepting it the way it is, everything's gonna be perfect." He patted me.

"Hang on. I'll just say hi to my friends inside and get back. I'll get my coffee."

"Nah that's alright. Go ahead. Join them." He said, looking at the inside of the coffee shop.

"That's ok, bud. We're going out together tonight. I can at least catch up with you for a while."

"Ok." He agreed with a smile. I walked in, told my friends that I'd join them in a while and they were fine with it. I looked at him smoking, as I waited for my bill at the counter. He was staring blankly at the cup with sadness. I felt like he was going to break down all of a sudden. I got my bill and was told that I'd be served at the table. I started

8

walking towards him through the door, feeling sorry for him. I walked past him towards my chair and he turned up to me with a sudden bright glorious smile.

"Where's your coffee?"

"They'll get it." I answered, amazed. "How do you do that?" I asked.

"Do what?"

"Never mind." I ignored. "What plans for the evening?" He smiled again.

Say no to heartbreaks

#1

Everybody's got a story. It's the way we narrate, that makes it beautiful, lively and most importantly, interesting. I have a story too; the story of my life, but mine is way too boring which can put even an imp to sleep. I'm a spoilt kid of a successful businessman and a beautiful house wife. My father was a senior software consultant for over 15 years in the United States of America where he trapped my mother with love and married her during her Master's program. They later gave birth to me, as significance to their love. It is from my parents, that I started to learn, what love is. From my mom kissing my dad, 'have a pleasant day' before he left to work. From my dad kissing me, 'don't get into trouble and have fun' before he dropped me off at school, every single day. From my dad's giving up his job and taking up a business back in India, so that mom could look after her dying father.

I'm currently pursuing my Masters education in New York City, United States of America, apart from spending my father's hard earned money in a bloody lavish manner.

All my friends are delinquent scum and trouble-making fools. We bunk classes together, hit the pubs, and later crash at my place, making the filthy apartment look filthier.

But this is not the story of my life. Neither my parents'. This is the story of a part of Tim Koster's life. The part which started from where he fell in love to God knows what happened of him. It took me more than a year to bring his story out from the dark. I had been chasing a ghost. I had been chasing the ghost of Tim Koster. I had been chasing the spirit of his love. I had been following the imaginary trail of bread crumbs he might have had left behind; in every place he had been.

Who is Tim Koster? I have no frigging clue. He was just a stranger to me until I met Mitali Rao at Fontana's bar, NYC, few years ago, when I just started my under graduation. I saw her from behind, as she ordered a drink at the bar. She was all alone, hopping her sexy coke bottle shaped body to David Guetta's trance music being played as the bartender fixed a drink for her. Taking a series of rhythmical steps towards her, synching with the music beat; I reached to her side and pretended to notice her abruptly. Storming a short balk look, she poured the drink off her glass down her throat, in a single gulp.

"I'm Vian." I shouted through the loud deafening music, for her, offering my hand for a shake. "Vian Bansi."

"Mitali." she shouted back, but her voice had dissolved into the music as she shook my hand with her soft and cold palms. I made a gentle gesture that I couldn't hear her and asked her to repeat whatever she said. "Mitali!" she shouted louder.

"Oh! Mitali." I smiled back, as she continued to hop

along with the music. "Boring, isn't it?"

She let out a cute, flattered smile, bent her face towards me and drawing her lips near to my ears, "I'm sorry to disappoint you, but it's not going to work." She shouted.

"Sorry I beg your pardon?" I shouted back with consternation. Her grey eyes added more beauty to her fair complexion, with her face covered on either side by her hair hanging loose.

"I'm here with my boyfriend." She screamed, as she retrieved and turned her eyes to our side at the dance floor. To my bewilderment, if it wasn't for Ryna, a friend and classmate of mine, I would have had a chance to have fun with Mitali and she wouldn't have remained my best friend as she is now.

"Son of a-", I exclaimed as Ryna approached us, jumping and dancing furiously with his glass hoisted above his head careful not to spill the drink.

"Is he hittin' on you?" he questioned her, giving me a cunning smirk. "Come on man. My girl too?" he turned to me.

"Asshole. I was just trying to make friends." I laughed, nodding for the bartender to fix drinks for us both, tossing Ryna's empty glass away.

"Yeah it starts with making friends and I know where it ends." He teased, adjusting his hair with his fingers. He has an athlete build with wheatish complexion, dark eyes, and always a cool look and confidence on his face; straight forward behavior.

"So I heard." Mitali mocked at me as we jogged our

way back onto the dance floor.

"Nah I'm kidding. He gets close with a girl, the moment he realizes that it's going to turn serious, he freaks out and runs away." Ryna said.

"Why is that?" Mitali asked him, looking at me.

"He's afraid of getting attached. After halfway, he chickens out." He laughed at me.

Ryna and Mitali had been friends since childhood back in India. Mitali chose to pursue her graduation in New York, and Ryna, without a thought tailed her all the way to New York and signed up for the same program as hers but in a different university, since he failed to get scholarship like Mitali did. Come to talk about it, finding a girlfriend in India is *really* easy. Keeping her, is the hardest part. An Indian girlfriend can cling on to her guy, as tight as a noose, or could slip right through the fingers like water. As for Ryna, he's a keeper. I was his first Indian friend in the US. Maybe we would have hated each other if we had met in India, but meeting a fellow Indian in a foreign country is more like running into a long lost brother.

It had been four years since I met Mitali but I wasn't aware that she was Tim Koster's best friend. Mitali and Tim were classmates during high school. Mitali was the only girl whom Tim didn't hit on. Nevertheless, her kind and crystal nature compelled between them, a bond of friendship. Tim was a NRI until his high school. He was born and brought up in UK, but had to continue his high school in India.

And I'm right here, in John F. Kennedy International airport, waiting for my flight to India. Unlike my previous journeys to India, I'm now travelling all alone; all alone without Mitali and Ryna, to keep me amused; to keep me too busy to feel jet-lagged. In three days from now, I will be meeting Tim's parents in India. I hope that I could find Tim Koster's whereabouts at least now. This would be my final tribulation in digging out Tim Koster's love story or better yet, his tragic love story.

It was about a year and a half ago, when my parents paid me a visit in New York; I threw a party at my place. Mom and dad's faces were marked with joy and pleasure as they spent time with me. Mom, just like any typical Indian housewife, always stuck to wearing traditional sarees. She's the most beautiful woman I've ever known I should say. Hair combed and tied, and she's about five feet ten just as my dad. Well dad, he's adaptable. His looks change according to situations. We argue and fight once in a while but we're best to each other.We had a family dinner planned along with Uncle Jamie Silburn, my mom's cousin. Handsome even in his early forties, few grey hair adding a little more glow to his face, always clean shaved and sharply dressed. I used to want to dress like him since I was a little boy. Uncle Jamie had been married to Deepa, my aunt,who is mom's second cousin, who later divorced him for some businessman in India. He had been living single since then, taking good care of his daughter. Dad came up with too many career plans for me which I later turned down. I convinced him that I wanted to live in the moment of a piece of life before I get settled in a serious manner. I however, always had the passion to write and spent most of my time, writing stories, songs and incomplete novels.

I started writing a short story to add to a collection one day, as I waited for mom and dad to return from shopping. Uncle Jamie walked in along with them in the evening and mom screamed from across the living room, for me to get dressed up for an early dinner so that I could later go crash at my party with friends. I traversed to the bathroom from my desk to take a quick shower and came out after about ten minutes. Uncle Jamie was going through my writings when I walked towards the shelf and pulled out a pair of formal clothes for dinner.

"Did you write these Vian?" he asked, staring at them as he stood beside my desk.

"Yep."

"How many more?" he questioned.

"About fifteen short stories, two-almost-novels and a lot of songs."

"I did not know that you write."

"I never had a chance to share them with anyone. It is more like a hobby to keep myself occupied."

"Occupied from what?" he asked, curiously with his eyes going through my work.

I paused for a second before closing the door of the wardrobe shelf staring blankly into it and held my breath. "Just to kill time." I lied, shutting the door and forced a smile as I looked at him.

"Did you know that I'm an editor in a major publishing company in New York?" he asked eagerly, turning his head to me, rather in a dubious manner.

"Yep."

"Do you mind if I take them home for a read?" He politely asked. "I have read one short story and it is very interesting."

"Perhaps, I can send them to you in an email?"

"Yeah, that would be great." He agreed, as mom hurried us out.

The silence in the car as dad drove, seemed unbearably dreadful to me. Meaningless thoughts crept in and started haunting my mind."Anita!" Uncle Jamie called, breaking the silence and turning back from the passenger seat to look at my mom who sat beside me at the back. "You never told me that your son writes?"

"Frankly, I didn't know too. I don't know anything about him, apart from his name and education, to begin with. He's been keeping to himself, lately." My dad answered, steering the wheel.

"Are you serious?" Uncle Jamie questioned. "You do not know that he writes? I read one short story and I can tell, that he's pretty good." He turned to me and passed me a smile.

"Thank you Uncle Jamie."

"Writing will help him kill time, but it won't help him live."

"Don't you start it, Varun! It's his passion. Besides, he's still studying. At least he's not getting drunk like the rest of the kids." Mom defended me.

"Mothers!" dad smirked as he drove, nodding disapprovingly.

"Dad, I wanna write about you." I started.

17

"What about me?"

"Let's sit some time. Tell me about any of your love stories before you found mom."

"Ok you know what? Let me be and I won't bother about your writing thingy ever again."

After a delicious dinner and wonderful time with family, I got back to my apartment to my friends and plunged into their way of fun. Mitali was sitting beside Ryna on couch and was teasing Tony as I fixed myself a drink.

"What did she say?" she was asking Tony and he was blushing.

"I don't know, but I think she will come." Tony answered.

I couldn't make out anything from that part of their conversation and gave Mitali a doubtful look. "He asked Lisa out for a date." She told me.

"Really?" I exclaimed. "You spoke to her after two years of just staring at her from like what, miles?"

"Come on man! It ain't that easy." Tony cut me off. "She's different. I'm in love with her."

"What is it with love and distance? If you love her, why can't you just talk to her?" I started.

"You will understand when it's your turn."

My phone had suddenly rung. It was Uncle Jamie. "Hello?"

"Vian! Did you reach home kid? I'm waiting for your

email."

"Oh! Yes, yes. I'll send you in a bit." I told him as I walked into my bedroom, hanging up on his call. As I walked away from the living room, Mitali and Tony's voices slowly faded and I could only hear the sound of the breeze through my bedroom window and distant honking and sounds of cars in the night traffic. I turned on my computer and emailed him a few of my short stories and two incomplete novels. I then returned back to the living room as I sent him a text to his mobile. *'Sent'*

I sat back with them and was listening to their crazy fun talk sipping on my beer. *'Got it.'* I received a reply.

Mitali was merrily taunting Tony and I was actually enjoying it. The vibration from her cell phone which was in her handbag was louder than the busy wailing night and the soft music from the stereo in a corner of the living room.

"Is that a China phone?" Tony teased, as she pulled it out. "That vibration is louder than my grandfather's snoring."

"Hello?" she answered, reaching out her leg to her front, to kick Tony but he dodged it. She listened to the caller in silence and her expression on the face changed abruptly. She then walked away, then turned down the stereo volume and continued to talk.

"Is it some new boyfriend? RYNA! Man, you're out." Tony continued. Mitali remained still listening to the caller in utmost silence and didn't bother to turn back to shut Tony up. In fact, she just rose up her hand to her side and gestured Tony to keep calm. Beginning to get the picture that it was something serious, Tony and I sat there without making a move, curious and equally worried what it could have been, while Ryna rose up to his feet and walked over to her. Noticing him approach, she passed over her phone to him and he continued to listen. I rose up forcibly to go over to her. I realized by then, that it was someone who was mutually known to them.

"Calm down, now. What's the condition?" Ryna asked, over the phone while Mitali leaned on to my shoulder and gripped my arm tightly.

"What's wrong?" I asked her in a whisper. Ryna was almost lost, in the conversation over the phone. Tony walked over to us too, uncertain of what to do. Mitali didn't utter a word but continued to stare at Ryna impatiently as he spoke.

"Ok. Calm down now. Nothing's going to happen. Just let him cool down. We shall think of something and work it out, alright? – Ok. Call me back."

"What the hell?" Mitali exclaimed, as he hung up the call.

"Don't worry. They keep doing that." Ryna calmed her down and took her back to the couch by her shoulder.

"What's wrong sweetie?" I asked again. She remained silent. She didn't speak. She couldn't.

"Tim Koster, one of our friends, his girlfriend broke up with him." Ryna answered me, running his palm on Mitali's head, as she leaned on his shoulder blankly.

"Oh! Huh! Come on. You guys made it look like that guy died." I eased.

"This is serious, Vian!" Mitali forced her head up and

spoke.

"Come on! You serious? This shit happens all the time." I began to debate, rising up back to my feet and walked towards the fridge. "You guys want another beer?" A sudden painful feeling jolted inside me and I could imagine what Tim would be going through, *if* he was really in love with his girlfriend.

"Yes." She let out a silent whisper, lost in her vocals. I gave them each a beer and settled back down. "For Tim, it is serious, Vian! You don't understand."

"No! You don't understand. When did she break up with him?"

"About few days ago." Ryna gave in.

"Then he'll go crazy today, he'll cry for a week or probably months, feel lonely later and finally he'll find another girl eventually.

"This is different, Vian." Ryna disagreed.

"How?" I questioned. "How is it different? How is this girl different from all the other stories from India you've told me?"

"This is how it goes." Ryna started. "He had been with a lot of girls before Saaya. He then went after Saaya. Now, she's not just any other girl. Traditional, sensitive, ethical, and believes in eternal relationship. They have been together for about four years now, and we were always frigging worried that he would dump her and break her. Apparently, she is the one who dumped him and is getting engaged soon."

"That's indeed, a different story." I remarked, with disappointment of losing the argument. "Was she truly in love with him?"

"Yes she was, but Tim might have seen that as a passing by affair, but he would never do anything that would hurt a girl. She was very kind-hearted. I wonder how she could do this! I mean Tim is a complicated guy. No one could understand him, but still, he's not a bad guy, that I can say."

Well, there's no answer to 'why or how.' No matter how kind the girl is, love gives her the strength to hurt. I walked towards the fridge to get myself another beer. Mitali's speech turned trenchant as she exaggerated about Tim's affliction, and her displeasure for what Saaya did. That pleasant night turned gloomy and sour after the news on phone. I tried to change the subject assuming that they'd be over it by morning. Tony did his best to divert the subject and made Mitali laugh again, but deep down, she had a planted disturbed feeling which was too heavy to come out of her face. Yes, probably they should be worried because it's choosing between two friends; Tim and Saaya.

"What's up with Tim and Mitali?" I asked Ryna in a whispering tone, at the balcony where he stepped out for a smoke.

"They're thick." He answered. "He always had her back. He was there for her when she had her first break up. Years went by, and they became great friends. And when I proposed to Mitali, Tim's opinion on me mattered a lot to her which helped her understand me and accept me into her life.It's hard to tell. Tim was always there when we needed him. If there's any man I'd trust blindly for Mitali to be with, it's Tim. I stood there staring at the city lights below us as he talked to me about Tim Koster. We went back in a while later and joined the others.

The next day, I was awoken by Uncle Jamie at half past four in the morning with a call to my cell phone. "Hello!" I answered with dragged up voice.

"Vian?" He spoke in a delirious tone. "You haven't sent me the remaining parts of your novels."

"You're still awake? And you have been reading my novels?" I asked him, surprised and my drowsiness partly fading away.

"I have read the fiction novel and noticed that the ending was missing in both of them. Anyway, I started the other crime novel but unable to help my inquisitiveness, I called you up."

"The previous end parts which I have written were not satisfactory, so I removed them. I couldn't write an end yet. They are incomplete." I told him, with a lowered voice.

"You must be joking. You have written them so well, and you're telling me that they are incomplete?" He questioned astonishingly.

"I'll finish them as soon as possible."

"Ok."

"Uh, er- Can we talk about this tomorrow? I'm terribly sleepy, I smell of beer and I have college in a few hours."

"Oh, yes yes. I'm sorry I woke you up." he apologized in a stuttering manner.

"It's alright. Get some sleep Uncle Jamie. I don't want you to be a second person wasting time on *my* writing."

Unable to fall back asleep, I lied down staring at the ceiling in my bedroom, thinking about the stories I have written. I have always been bad at shaping an end to the story. Perhaps, I needed to contribute more determination. My passion for writing was not adequate enough. I felt resentful at my incapability of writing a perfect ending. All the same, I was occupied with the hopeless thoughts of the girl I was in love with; Tianna, whom my dad looked upon as his own daughter; plausibly, because he always wanted a girl child, but I was born a boy. I was in love with her while she was only in a relation with me for about three years until she fell for a celebrated music artist. I realized that my love was my weakness, and her strength. It's been a year since I began to endure the pain it caused, and confronted with the suffering. If it wasn't for my dad and mom, I would have had a very hard time. Unlike most other typical Indian parents, they understood me better than anyone else and helped me get out of that phase. My parents now long for me to complete my Masters, so that they can get me married.

Ryna was jabbering off by the time I arrived at college the following morning. I received a text message to my phone at 10 am from Uncle Jamie asking if I could meet him after college. I agreed and he invited me to dinner at Blue Hill restaurant at 75, Washington, NYC. After a routine day at college, I was driving my way back home when Uncle Jamie called.

"Hello?" I answered, steering with my left hand.

"You didn't forget about our meeting tonight, did you?" he reminded.

"Of course I didn't. I will be there." I assured.

"Good! See you at dinner then."

I freshened up, watched TV for a while and did some writing. I killed the evening with my attempts in vain, to write an end to my novels. My perturbed mind didn't cooperate with me after which I managed to write a very good short story. I took a glance at my watch to check the time and I noticed that I was late. I was due to meet Uncle Jamie in fifteen minutes and it was a half hour drive. I drove as fast as I could, abiding by the traffic rules. I wished I was in India, so I could break as many traffic rules as possible. Somehow, I managed to arrive at the restaurant in twenty and let the valet, dressed in neat dark brown over coat jacket over a white shirt and black trouser at the bottom, park my car. Fortunately, Uncle Jamie was just being directed to the table he reserved and I joined him before he could take a seat.

"Oh!" he exclaimed surprised. "I reckoned you were going to turn up late."

"Then you are wrong." I mocked him as I settled down opposite to his chair. "So, is it anything important?"

"It depends." He answered, going through the menu in his hand. I looked into the menu as well. "I'll make it simple." He started after I finished with ordering the food. "Have you considered getting your novels published?"

"I have made a few attempts." I answered, smiling away.

"But you failed to complete the stories?"

"I try my best, but I am just not able to complete

25

them. Haven't you slept? You look weary."

"I liked your novels Vian. I'm still reading the other novel for now. If you finish your novels and submit to me the complete manuscripts, I shall perhaps consult with my team and see what I can do.

"I will do my best. Just give me a few days' time." I agreed.

"You will have to take this seriously. Stay low this weekend and complete your manuscripts. I am queerly filled with suspense by your incomplete novels. I will look forward to your completing them so that I can read the climax." He said.

"Ok. No hanging out this weekend. I'll sit back and finish 'em." I promised him. We had a pleasant dinner talking about other stuff and walked out saying good nights.

Later that night, after reaching home, I turned on my PC and sat down to continue writing my story. I felt tired, slightly drowsy, my feet tapping the cold floor beneath me while I tried to type. After two hours I was graveled to notice that I had only typed one page for so long. Making up my mind to type more the next morning, I crashed onto my bed and fell asleep. I spent the following days tampering my brain as I tried to complete my novels. I was afraid that perhaps I was not destined to write. I tried to motivate myself by listening to music, taking a walk through the evening's cool breeze, spending time in beautiful locations, but nothing was of any help. I started to feel like writing was my hypothetical passion. The weekend came and passed by, like rains in India. I ran out of the time I was given by Uncle Jamie. Filled with agitation, I rang him up.

"I couldn't do it. I couldn't complete them." I stammered.

"What's wrong?" he questioned.

"I couldn't finish the stories." I blurted, walking into the balcony from my bedroom at the dead of the night.

"Do you have anything else that we can consider for evaluation?" he asked. "If we like it, we shall discuss and let you know."

"I have a collection of short stories."

"Short story collection is not a good idea for now. Evaluation, production and promotion will be beneficial if it is a novel. Do you have any other novels? A complete manuscript?"

"Umm no." I answered disapprovingly.

"What shall we do? Hmm- Er." he murmured, as he thought. "Ok. How about, you write a new one? Write a love story. It should be easy for you considering your age and friends."

"I don't know, should I? I'll give it a thought." I agreed, hesitantly.

"Even if you put hundred percent of your effort we might just like it but reject it. If you want it through, your story should be beyond our expectations and most importantly, the ending should be Godly. It should not be superfluous. I can only guide you and the decision lies with the editorial team in our company. I need you to understand that." He explained, in a commanding, yet conciliatory manner.

"Give me some time." I asked and he agreed. "My vacations will be starting in a week and I'll finish something then."

"Alright."

I went to sleep early, disturbed by the thoughts about my incomplete novels. I decided to finish the fantasy story I have written about a man and his magic staff, since Uncle Jamie liked it anyway. 'Love stories are routine. Everyone can write them. What difference does it make if I write another?' I thought.

I continued noting down a few key points in the classroom the next morning, about the story and the adventures in 'The man with the magic staff.' The continuation of the story that I have framed didn't look fair enough. I wanted to take a break before I persevere with typing the novel. I called in for a party that night at my home and we had a small gathering for dinner and drinks. Mitali cooked some Indian food while Tony ordered for pizza as well. Tony started to blabber about his girlfriend while we drank up the beer and listened with patience, Ryna teasing him, pretending to yawn, and giving Tony an idea that he was boring us. I told them about Uncle Jamie's suggestion and they were all equally excited and curious.

"So your novel will get out soon." Ryna remarked. "Get that story with the staff out first. I loved it, even though you didn't complete it."

"I'm working on it." I said, sipping on my beer.

"What happened with Tim Koster?" Tony asked Mitali all of a sudden. "Is he alright now?"

"Oh! I forgot to tell you." She started with a

saddened, deplorable face. "He met with an accident day before yesterday and he's in ICU now. We'll be seeing him when we go to India for vacation."

"What the-?" Tony exclaimed. "How?" I was shocked myself and I had a strange feeling deep in my guts.

"He went on a rash drive, drove off the road and his car tumbled over." Mitali and Ryna's faces bore disappointed expressions which clearly showed how much they loved Tim Koster.

Later, cutting out of Tim Koster's topic, she gave Tony suggestions on how to talk to Lisa or where to take her. I listened to her childish ideas as I stared into the gleam in Tony's eyes. I saw in Tony, myself, few years ago when I was in love with Tianna. I slowly drifted into her memories. All the memories of crazy fun I had with her, romantic dinners and drives, blurred my vision. "Why don't you come with us, Vian?" Mitali asked all of a sudden drawing my attention towards her.

"What?"

"Why don't you come with us to India for the vacation? Ryna will get busy with his family get together and I will be bored. We can hang out and have some fun." She suggested.

"Yes, Vian! Why don't you come with us? That way she'll be busy eating your head rather than mine." Ryna teased and Mitali punched his belly with her elbow making him groan.

"Uh- er- I have to stay back and complete my novels by vacation." I denied.

"Come on. You can write at my home. It's a peaceful atmosphere unlike the noise of the traffic here." She pushed, putting up puppy dog eyes.

"We have one week at hand. We shall plan." I hesitated.

#2

I spent the following days, living in exceptionally replete intellections. I paid no attention to anything that people said. I fed my hunger on cogitated ideas about my novel. I craved for more composition of themes and plots.

I was preoccupied with weird thoughts one night which gave me a very difficult time sleeping. That weird thoughts dissolving inside my head, my heart beat rate grew rapid and louder. Taking up my cell phone from the table beside my bed, I sent a text message to Mitali, then waited till the sun came up, holding my anxiety, and rang up to Uncle Jamie.

"Hello?" he answered drowsily.

"Didn't wake up yet?" I asked.

"What time is it? Did I oversleep? What is it?" he burbled.

"I need you to wake up to your senses." I said. His

caring voice reminded me of my childhood when he used to come over for the weekends, just to play with me.

"Mmmm. Ok." He moaned in a sluggard manner. "Yes. Tell me now."

"I'm going to India this weekend for the vacation." I blurted out.

"What? I thought you said you would finish your novel." He asked, intensely shocked. "I want you to take this seriously, Vian."

"I know. Just give me two months. I will get you the story. I promise." I requested.

"Two months?" he asked. "Are you sure?"

"Yes."

"Ok. Have a good time." He said and hung up. I took a shower, had my brunch as I was late to college and drove away. Just as any other routine day, I sat through all the classes, waiting for them to end. I rushed out with Ryna in the evening as he was in hurry to pick up Mitali. She was just heading out of her classes when we parked our cars.

"Where are we going?" she asked as I got out of my car and walked to Ryna's.

"Vian's place." He said, getting out of his car. "And he's coming to India with us for the vacation."

"You sure about it?" Mitali asked, as I approached them.

"Yes. I need a change. Mom and dad have a slight busy schedule here anyway. I could pay a visit to my grandparents." I assured her.

"Ok. Book the tickets for the three of us then." She snapped and grinned at us. I gave her a simper look, then pulled out my phone and called dad.

"Dad? I'm going to India with Mitali and Ryna for vacation." I informed.

"Sudden plan?" he asked.

"Kind of."

"Ok. Be back early so that we can spend time with you before we leave." He ordered.

"Ok. Book tickets for the three of us then." I asked him, hung up the call and grinned back at Mitali before walking back to my car.

"You're such a-"

"Thank you." I teased.

I gave a break to writing, preceding the vacation plan. I decided to frame and compile a story during the vacation, then return back to New York and finish it. We spent the next few days shopping and buying gifts for friends and relatives in India. That's what most families in India expect when someone comes from overseas. We had a small party two days before the day of our journey. Mom and dad joined us too.

"How far along are you with Lisa?" dad asked Tony all of a sudden and Tony, shocked and surprised, shot an angry glare at me. I shrugged my shoulders with raised eyebrows and avoided eye contact with him, pretending to look into the bottom of the bottle of beer in my hand. Mom was busy serving us food as we sat there in the living room of my apartment and chatted. "Did you propose to her yet?"

Tony shook a no, and continued with his drink, helping himself to the roasted chicken on the table.

"Make it special." Dad suggested, eating off the spoon, the dessert which mom gave him. "When you love someone, you say it. The longer you hold yourself back, the farther she goes."

The following day, I got busy with packing my luggage and prepared for the journey. Mom and dad spent the night with me to drop us at the airport the next day. Mitali and I would be staying in Mumbai in India, while Ryna would go over to Bangalore to his folks. We had to check in two hours early, so we parted from my parents as mom kissed me. The wait wasn't boring. It was rather fun with shopping in the airport, checking out beautiful girls and airhostesses around, food stalls, and more shopping. Mitali and Ryna looked mirthful, but they had the vague nervousness buried within their faces. At that instant of time, I somehow knew that they would not be themselves again, until they saw Tim Koster.

After a pleasant flight, we were heartily welcomed and received by Mitali's parents. Mr. Rao looked old and weary than the last time I had seen him. Dressed in simple casual shirt, he almost cried as Mitali ran to him and hugged him hard like a small girl.

"How are you boys?" he asked, looking at Ryna and me.

"We're fine. How are you?" Ryna greeted back.

We had a very pleasant conversation on our way to Mitali's home. Ryna and I were shown into a guest room while Mrs. Rao hugged and kissed Mitali in the living room with her Indian type of love.A whilelater, I was taking a shower, trying to be intrepid, while Tianna's thoughts daunted my consciousness.

"Hurry up Vian!" I heard Mitali's voice from outside the bathroom, from within the guest room we were in. "We have to go over to Tim's."

"In a minute." I shouted back and pulled the towel from the hanger. As I dressed up, I could hear Mitali's voice from distant, in the living room, talking to her dad. He agreed to drive us to Tim's home. We got into the car as Mitali took the front seat. Come a little early before you guys return to New York, Ryna. I would like to show you around to our relatives.

"Sure, uncle." Ryna agreed.

"I spoke to your father about the engagement. I somewhat pushed him a bit on this, and he said he'd check with the dates. You have to try and understand that I'm the girl's father." He explained, taking glances at Ryna through the rear view mirror. "Few mouths in our family are not too good and trustworthy."

Ryna chuckled and, "Don't worry about it uncle. I'll talk to dad as well. I was thinking I'd get a job first, but we shall go ahead with what you feel better." He assured.

The conversation propelled me into the memories of my past. Tianna and I were kids back then. Every time our families met, she would come hopping for me and we would wander off into our world and play. Our parents wanted us

35

to get married when we grew up. When Tianna's dad would ask me if I would marry her, I used to coy away and look at her. "Tell him that you'd marry me if he gives you lot of toys. And I will marry you if you agree to share them with me." She would squeak in a tone of whisper. As we grew up, we became fond of each other. We would ask our parents to have a family get together more often so that we could spend more time together and they would tease us that they'd get us married right away.

"Vian?" I heard a muffled voice from somewhere deep inside my head; someone calling for me in a dream, or from inside my memories. "Vian?"

"VIAN!" I heard it again, louder and clearer. It was Mitali trying to draw my attention. I then noticed her dad looking at me in the rear view mirror as he drove and slowly realized that the muffled voice belonged to him.

"Yes, uncle?" I answered his call, rather too late but politely. "I'm sorry my mind was carried away with something.

"Don't worry. It's been a long time since you last came to Mumbai. How do you like it now?" he asked with his most pleasant smile.

"I love it, no matter how long it's been." I answered.

"How's mom and dad?" he asked, with his eyes on the road.

"They're great as usual." I blushed. "They are in New York, attending dad's friend's wedding and enjoying a long holiday."

"Good." He remarked. "You never told me that you

36

write?"

"That's something I took up to distract my mind from something else, but it grew to be my passion." I said.

"I'm waiting for your stories to get out."

"Me too." I smiled away though he wasn't looking at me.

After what seemed like a long drive in a hectic polluted Indian traffic, we reached Tim Koster's house and pulled the car onto the parking beside the street. Mitali, worried and excited to see Tim, dashed out, kicking the door open, like a mad dog let out of a cage. She raced to the heavy main gate and sunk with disappointment at the sight of the lock on the gate. She looked around for a while as we walked towards her at the gate.

"It's locked." She said with a frown. Ryna took a few steps towards the neighbor's compound and shouted out for someone from a distant.

"Excuse me? Any idea where the Kosters are?"

After a long pause and silence, someone opened the gate and stepped out. We went over to find out where they had gone, and, "They have been away for a few days now." An old man in early sixties, dressed in his casuals answered. "You are-?"

"I'm Ryna." He introduced himself. "These are my friends Vian and Mitali, and he's my uncle, Mr. Rao. We're here for Tim Koster." We greeted him as we neared him, and he put up a doubtful expression on his face.

"So, any news about Timmy?" he questioned, looking

at Mr. Rao.

"What do you mean?" Ryna questioned back.

"Well, the poor boy is missing." He said, in a wavering manner.

"What happened?" Mr. Rao gave in. He tried to convince the old man, to tell us the truth without any hesitation.

"After the accident, he was kept in ICU for two days and the next morning, he went missing." The old man averred.

"Where did he go?" Mitali asked worried.

"We wouldn't call it missing if we knew where he went, would we?" he said, staring at us through his wrinkly eyes.

"Have they looked for him?" Ryna questioned, as I looked away at Tim's house, trying to examine.

"I have no idea. Kosters don't talk much after that." He let out a sad grin, looking down at the ground. He walked back inside murmuring within himself. Walking back towards the car, Mitali made a few calls and inquired about Tim.

"Dad! Let's go to the hospital. I'll drive." She spoke falteringly, as she hurriedly got behind the steering wheel. It took her fifteen minutes to reach the hospital. Sheapplying the brakes hard and parked the car in the cellar of the hospital building. Mr. Rao didn't utter a word because he was equally worried as we were.

"Where can I find Dr. Aman?" she asked, at the reception.

"Please follow the stairs to the first floor and you will find him in the emergency ward." The receptionist answered her politely, pointing her pen at the stairs behind us. Ryna hit the stairs before Mitali and they hurried together as Mr. Rao and I tried to keep up with them. After searching and asking around for a few minutes, a doctor in white coat answered Ryna that he was the one they have been looking for. He looked young, clean shaved, about six feet high, fairly looking in his white apron and stethoscope in his hands.

"Do you remember Tim Koster? He was under your observation few days ago." Ryna asked him.

"Yes." The doctor exclaimed horrified. "Did you find him?"

"We were hoping you'd tell us something. One of my friends told me that you were the last one who saw him." Mitali interfered.

"He seemed like a hard guy. He was brought in, in a very bad shape. He didn't make any sound while I stitched his cuts and dressed his wounds." The doctor started. "I gave him a sedative the night before the day he went missing, to put him to sleep. I received a call from one of my staff members the next morning that he was nowhere to be found. We informed his parents right away, and that's all I know." He finished.

"How bad was he?" Mr. Rao asked.

"Very. We did whatever we could to find him. I have contacted all the other hospitals and gave them a description to keep us informed of any possible casualty." He accounted.

Cast into perfect silence, I sat there in the back seat of the car, while Ryna, Mitali and Mr. Rao fell into stupefaction. Their faces displayed dazed expressions. It showed how much they loved Tim Koster. I was slightly worried too. There was nothing we could do to find him. There was nowhere we could go. There was no one we could turn to for help. Everyone who knew about Tim Koster's tragedy has the exact same amount of information; that he went missing.

The in-frangible silence at the dinner table that night was broken by Mr. Rao. "Don't worry. I'm sure he's fine. Give him a while. He'll come back. He's stronger than we think he is."

"I'm worried, dad." Mitali spoke. "We don't have a single clue. I tried reaching his parents too but their phones are switched off."

"Calm down, sweetie!" Ryna tried. "He's gonna be fine."

Mitali shook her head disapprovingly and continued trying to gulp down the food which seemed to have stuck at her throat. It was as if her food pipe narrowed down, riled no end by the fate of Tim Koster.

"Mr. Rao? Could you let us borrow your car for Vian to drop me at the airport in the morning? I will have to leave early." Ryna requested, looking at him, holding Mitali's hand, to calm her down.

"Oh! I'll drop you myself. Perhaps we can have a chat." Mr. Rao offered.

"Are you sure you want to wake up that early?"

Ryna asked.

"No problem." He said and continued to eat. Silence fell over again except for the clattering of spoons and forks.

I was sound asleep to even notice Ryna leave. I woke up late in the morning to the aroma of the coffee by the bedside table, and found out that Ryna had left. Picking up the coffee cup, I walked out to the living room where Mr. Rao was reading the newspaper. "Good morning, Mr. Rao." I wished as I settled on a sofa. "Ryna left?"

"Good morning." He wished back. "Yes I just dropped him at the airport and returned few mins back. Slept well?"

"Yes." I answered and Mitali appeared all dressed up traditional to my surprise. "Now I understand why he ran away."

Hitting my head with her hand, she settled down beside Mr. Rao and, "Mom! Coffeeee!" she shouted.

"Doesn't she look beautiful in this dress Vian? She always prefers jeans and tees I wonder why." Mr. Rao commented.

"Yes she does." I agreed, sipping my coffee. "Our driver will pick me up later this morning. Will go check how my grandparents are doing and will get back tomorrow."

"Ok. Good. Convey my regards to them." Mr. Rao said.

"Come back soon. I'll get bored." Mitali squeaked.

"Trust me; the only thing she is going to do is

shopping. Be wise and take your time." Mr. Rao joked. My driver parked the car by the gate and rang me up. Hurrying myself, I got dressed after a quick shower and left.

"How are you, sir?" he asked as I got in beside him throwing my bag onto the rear set.

"I'm fine. How are you?"

"I'm good too." He smiled. "How was the flight?"

"It was alright. Bring your kids along in the evening. I got something for them." He gave me a nod and drove away towards my grandparents' home. It was an hour drive from Mitali's home.

My old folks were beaming as they eagerly waited for me. Grandma gave me a warm hug and grandpa rose up from his chair. He was dressed in polo tees and shorts. His hair was all white and wrinkles conquered his face. "Let me try and lift you in my arms. It's been ages since I carried you around." He said, slightly bending his knees and wrapping his arms around me to lift me up. Goodness me! He wasn't too old to lift me up. Sweet Indian dishes for lunch and loving talk with them, made my day. We sat there outside in the garden in the evening, playing with our driver's kids, when Uncle Kishore drove in through the gate. I could recognize his old classic car anywhere in the world. Greatly surprised and puzzled, as he got down the car, he looked at me and walked towards us with uncertainty, his eyes fixed upon me.

My grandparents' faces devolved from gleaming happiness to uncomfortable looks, as he approached us. "How are you Vian? Surprised to see you here." He said taking a seat with us.

"Fine, thank you. I'm pretty surprised too." I said, pretending to be polite. "How's Tianna?"

"I'm here to invite you to her wedding." He said with a frozen tone, looking at my grandpa, and turning to me, "You should come as well without fail."

I choked out on words and was washed out of emotions. I failed to react to what he said. My heartbreak turned severe, although it happened long ago from then. Tianna broke up with me saying Uncle Kishore didn't want us to get married and she wouldn't tell me the reason. The relations between our families turned sour and we haven't met lately after that incident. My dad and mom were pretty furious since that break up damaged me a lot and they hated to see me in that situation. Dad felt the necessity that Uncle Kishore should have at least talked about it upfront instead of chickening out like that. I was always doubtful that it was Tianna who was trying to break away.

"Could I borrow Vian for a while?" he requested my grandpa and I got up to walk with him to his car.

"Vian! I don't know what happened between you two, but it created quite a distance between our families. As her father, I cannot force her to marry you." he went on.

An outrageous whim to question him blew up in my mind but I forced myself to keep calm. "She told me that *you* didn't want her to marry me." I blurted out. He dropped his jaw and looked at me with a twisted face.

"You had a mutual breakup, didn't you?" he questioned me back and he sounded just as furious and astonished as I was.

"She broke up with me. I didn't." I answered sternly.

He continued to gaze at me with a puzzled expression. "She did it. I didn't even agree. She ended it with one single phone call. As if it were one of the games we used to play when we were kids back then and she just needed a phone call to call it off." I enraged.

"Vian!" he called. "I'm truly sorry. I was not aware of what happened. I was with a misconception that you didn't get along well, and it led to the distance between our families. She shouldn't have done it this way." I could see the disappointment and feeling of regret in his face. The grievance caused by Tianna's dashing hopes was clearly visible through his eyes. "I will talk to her."

"Let her be." I scoffed.

"We can't let this slip." He argued.

"I'm not bothered anymore. Now that you know the truth, I shall let it pass. Tenably, she thought of me as boring. She is marrying a musician, isn't she? He is possibly livelier than me and rich too. I'm glad she found someone better." I spoke in a storming tone. Losing control on his mind, bowing his head down with regret, he silently waddled to his car, got in and drove away. I realized that I exaggerated like a child and felt embarrassed, watching his car roll away out through the gate. Why would I even try to compare myself with someone else? If that was Tianna's choice, so be it.

"Where did he get the nerve to face us?" grandma muttered as I walked back to them.

"It wasn't his fault." I defended. "She lied to us." I sat down on the chair and stared at the table as grandma served tea. I failed to pay attention to any of their talk for a while.

My hands shivered with unbelief and my head stirred. I felt like I needed a vigorous shake of head to get back to normal. I managed to conceal the sadness as I looked down, to prevent my grandparents from cursing Tianna.

They couldn't ignore but attend the wedding the next day, for the sake of the self-respect of our families. Why hurt Tianna's parents when it wasn't their fault! I was left all alone that night, demented and broke. Falling asleep seemed to be the most impossible task. Her memories stung my head like sharp needles. I strongly wanted to go and scream at her at the top of my lungs, but I decided to let her live with the choice she made. I presumed that mom and dad heard from my grandparents, when they continuously rang me to my mobile. I answered mom's call after about five rings and kept my voice very still. I hung up abruptly telling her that I'd talk to her the next day. Uncle Jamie called me after a few minutes and I broke down into a silent cry. "Calm down, Vian!" he said in a soothing tone.

"I'm fine." I lied.

"She doesn't know what she missed." He said.

"She is better off without me." I sobbed.

"She missed you. She failed to preserve a great guy." He supported.

"She found someone better. She shouldn't have been with me when she was going to find someone else better." I continued to cry. No matter where I was born and raised, that childish Indian grief of a heartbroken man was sound alive inside me.

"You are an author." He reminded me, patiently.

45

"When she broke up she told me life with him was lively, and that she loved him for his voice. I suck at writing." I spoke in a childish manner, trying to join all the broken words amongst my sobs.

"His music may be heart touching, lively, and entertaining. But words are far more powerful than anything else. They have the magic in them to inspire, to motivate, to create a furor, the strength to convince, stop wars and bring peace, to make someone fall in love; words have the power to create revolution, and you can write." He debated, without a pause. "If there's anyone who thinks you are boring; they can talk to me." He thrust some zeal into me, and I listened to him as I tried to control my sobs. "You there?"

"Yes." I whispered.

"I won't ask you to stop crying. Cry your way to sleep. Wake up fresh tomorrow. Have fun with friends. Take your time. As much time as you might want. You can give me the story when you're done. I promise you to give you the importance you have lost. Why would I even bother to ask for your stories if you suck at writing? Trust me. Just believe in yourself. Never lose faith. Never lose hope. You can never gain them back once you lose them. Alright?"

"Ok." I answered.

"Drink plenty of water and go to sleep. Your girlfriend is probably waiting." He joked.

"I don't have a girlfriend." I denied.

"Now, I know you have a crush on some girl in your class. Your dad told me." He teased, which made me smile. He hung up the call after I wished him good night and I fell asleep in no time, from the achein my eyes.

My grandparents returned from wedding somewhere after midnight while I was asleep. I saw Tianna's face in my dreams and woke myself up as if she were a nightmare. I tried falling asleep again, trying to shut my eyes on her face. I tossed and turned around on the bed, as if I was turning away from her. I eventually fell asleep and woke up very late the next day. The burning sun was heating up my body through the window. I woke up and walked over to draw the curtains but unable to sleep again, I freshened up and went out of the bedroom to leave to Mitali's place.

"Come pay us a visit again before you leave." Grandpa asked.

"Crazy kid! He can't spend a few days with us." Grandma complained.

"I'll come back." I assured, kissing her on her cheek. "I just want to go around and meet some friends."

I sat in the car on the way to Mitali's home thinking about Tianna and trying to constrict my feelings for her. No matter how hard I tried, I could not erase her off of my mind. She remained a hard stain in my heart and her memories dissolved into the walls of my brain. My attempts to kill the retentions of the past went in vain. I felt that she had the right to choose her way of life; only if she had done that in a better way; in a way which didn't hurt anyone.

I was made to have lunch again in Mitali's home although my tummy was full. "Any news about Tim?" I asked as she served me with dessert.

"Not yet." She answered disappointingly. "We're going to meet some of my college friends now. Hope we pick something up."

"I don't have many friends from around here; only very few whom I made during my holiday visits. So I won't be eating much time. Let's look for Tim." I suggested.

I let Mitali drive the car since I lost track of all the routes in Mumbai. Receding myself into Tianna's thoughts, I wished things had happened in a different manner. I thought about the possibilities of us remaining just friends. I thought about the possibilities of my living in India in my past, so the long distance relation wouldn't have had the chance to break us apart. I was deeply lost in her thoughts when Mitali parked the car near cafe coffee day at Pali Hill. She was to meet one of her classmates in there who had already been waiting for us. She was of medium build, black hair and fair complexion.

"Hey!" Mitali greeted her with a hug and introduced her to me.

"Daphne. Vian. Vian. Daphne."

We settled down and ordered coffee as they had a casual talk before getting straight to the point. "Do you know where Tim is?" Mitali asked.

"I heard about the accident. I hope he's fine now." Daphne answered innocently.

"Oh! Yeah!" Mitali cut the topic; getting the picture that Daphne knew nothing.

"Anil was here until a while ago with his friends. He might know something." Daphne suggested.

"Do you have his number?" Mitali asked.

"Yeah." Daphne pulled out her mobile from her handbag and dialed. "Hey how far have you gone? – Yeah can you come back? – Mitali is here too. -Ok, bye." She hung up the call. "He'll be here in ten."

"I'll introduce you to a funny character." Mitali giggled, looking at me. "He's our senior. Cool guy, but always gets into funny situations." Mitali and Daphne started laughing together and it looked like they just got out of a crack house, since I wasn't aware of whatever reason they were laughing at.

After about fifteen minutes, Mitali looked behind Daphne at a guy with an athlete body build, who was heading to the door from the outside. He had dark brown eyes which suited best to his smiling face. Noticing us seated in the room, he walked over, joyfully.

"Hey Mitali! Long time. When did you come? Where's Ryna?" he greeted, taking a seat beside Daphne. "Hi I'm Anil!" he gave his hand forward for a shake. I took it and,

"Vian!" I said.

"You haven't changed at all, have you?" Mitali questioned him.

"How long are you staying?" he asked her.

"We should be returning in a month." She answered. "Hey! Do you know where Tim is?"

"Huh Tim?" he jeered.

"Yeah." Mitali wizened her eyes.

"I'm sorry. You know we don't get along very well. My friends joined him in the hospital and that's the last I've heard." He said. "No hard feelings."

"Let's go order something to eat." Daphne pulled Mitali by her arm and they left to the counter.

"So what do you do?" Anil asked me. "How do you know Mitali?"

"Oh! Ryna is my classmate and I know her through him." I answered, smiling back.

"They're such a sweet pair man, I'll tell you that. And strong." He remarked.

"What is it about you didn't get along well with Tim Koster? You can tell me if you don't mind." I asked him politely.

"Oh, it's just that he's arrogant. He popped up a fight with us his very first day at college." He started.

"How?"

"Here in India ragging is a part of tradition or custom in college life. Usually we try and have a funny conversation and make friends. Sometimes, people cross a few lines in the process. Lately, the Government has framed it to be an act of crime. And Tim Koster, had an attitude problem." He went on, until he was interrupted by Mitali.

"Don't be so mean." She cut him off, taking their seats back with plates of sandwiches in their hands.

"Come on. Let him go on." I pleaded, curiously.

"It was our second year. We were excited to rag

50

juniors like our seniors did to us. He drove in, in a Mercedes back then, and had a captivating appearance. He saw us ragging other students and ignored us, like he was passing by a road show.

"Over here! Junior!" one of my friends called for him.

"Heh! In your dreams." He barbed and continued to walk away with a disgusted look on his face. We crossed his path and blocked him. We asked him to perform one of his talents for us, and unless he entertained us, we weren't going to let him go.

"I'm very good at directing people's fingers up their arseholes. Who wants to volunteer?" he mocked, and insulted us. One of us caught his collar with rage, but Koster kicked him in the stomach with his knee and it lead to a fight and a threatened warning from the principal, since Koster's mouth was slightly bleeding along with two of us hurt.

"I'm warning you as well Mr. Koster. If you so much as repeat this arrogance again-" the principal warned him, but,

"I don't give a damn as long as they don't cross my path. Or anyone for that matter. I will bow and face consequences if I'm found guilty, sir." Koster cut him off. Bloody NRI was arrogant as crazy." Anil continued to loathe.

"Come on, Anil!" Mitali snarled. "Why do you hate him?"

"He has problem with everything. He's a womanizer." Anil continued, despite Mitali warning him.

"He just gets along well. It wasn't his fault. Most of them were materialistic and he was filthy rich." She fended for Tim.

"He's nothing but trouble and pain in the-"

"He's frigging missing." Mitali let out a lowered muttering shout, trying not to draw too much attention.

"What?" Anil snapped with a tempest shock.

"He went missing about a week ago. We have no clue how to contact him." She said and narrated to him all that she knew. "It's been a very long time since I left India and I don't know where to search for him."

"I'll ask around and see what I can do." Anil gave in, and we got up to leave the cafe. "But I still don't like him, man." He whispered to me cunningly.

"Vian!" Mitali called as she drove to Kosters'. "I'm terribly worried. Do you think he's alright?"

"Yes, babe. Don't you worry now! Let's go check his home." I smoothly said but it was no solace to her.

"He better be home." She chanted. We approached Kosters' and Mitali pulled the car over to the parking area beside the road, but didn't stop the engine to get out. She stayed stuck to the seat, disappointed, at the sight of the locks on the gates. "Shit!" she screamed, resting her forehead on the steering with a thump. I held her hand with mine and tried to keep her calm. "I hope he's ok" she grumbled.

"She's upset." I told Uncle Rao back at the house as he saw Mitali's fried face and turned to me in a questioning manner.

"Yes." Mr. Rao agreed, staring blank at the floor as he sat on the couch. "Koster was Mitali's best friend. He was there for her right at the time when she needed someone and he helped her out better than any of us did. I trusted him with no other girl but my very own daughter. I don't know, I just had faith in him that my daughter was safe with him no matter what. He brought Mitali and Ryna together. I fell in love with him then. I wished I had a son like him." he said, looking sadly at the floor.

"He will be fine, uncle. Just don't worry." I said.

"Wonder what happened to that poor guy. Saaya was an angel. She was his cure and remedy. I feel sorry for her." He went on and paused for a while. "Go to sleep, now. You must be tired. I don't want to manipulate your vacation mood now."

"That's alright, uncle. I would like to blend in and help you guys find him." I said. He gave me a thankful adorable look and walked away, wearily, to his bedroom.

I lied flat on the bed, listening to songs and checking notifications on my Facebook profile. I searched for Tim Koster and browsed his profile. He put a photograph of Saaya and himself as his profile picture. They looked beautiful together. His album contained mostly of Saaya's pictures with him. I went through his timeline scrolling down, and Saaya liked and commented on every post of Tim's. Tim Koster and Saaya Viroodh posted on each other's timeline often, teasing each other, fighting, playing, with their whole caboodle of love hidden in their talk. I browsed Saaya Viroodh's profile and she had an image of her engagement as her profile picture. I went through her album and there wasn't a single picture of Tim Koster. Was removing the memories of a person we love that easy, as deleting the pictures? My eyelids started to feel very heavy and I put my mobile aside to get to sleep. The next thing I remember was the scent of delicious coffee on the bedside table. I wondered who put it there every morning. It was more of a wakeup call to me.

#3

I found Mitali wrapped up in a blanket that protected her from the morning cold and locking in, the laziness, as she sipped her coffee. "What happened to your face?" I asked, noticing a painful expression on it.

"Fever!" she whined. Settling down beside her, I touched her forehead and it gave me a freaking feeling that she took it out of a furnace.

"What happened all of a sudden?" I asked, but she was busy drinking her coffee.

"I crept onto her bed to give her a surprise and noticed she had a fever." I heard a girly voice coming out of the kitchen. I turned my head towards it and Daphne walked towards us.

"Hey! Good morning." I wished.

"Good morning." She said back in a tonal pattern,

trying to be sweet.

"Vian, I'm worried about Tim." Mitali started.

"He's gonna be fine. He will certainly come back. It could all be a plot. His parents probably could have taken him somewhere to a different world to cool him off for a change after they found him. In this new world, he would be exploring a different kind of hope." I theorized.

"I need to be sure about it." She pushed. "You and your stupid theories."

"We shall find him. Don't worry. Just stay calm and take rest."

"We're going to meet Anil. He's going to help us." Mitali said.

"No. Stay back and take rest. Daphne and I will go with him." I suggested.

"Ok." She agreed and laid down her coffee mug and raked her fingers through her hair.

I went back into the bedroom to get ready. Mrs. Rao prepared breakfast by the time I got out. We ate it up as I listened to Mitali's instructions on whom to meet, how to talk, et cetera. I knew friends could be so attached together but the love Mitali had for Tim, I felt he was more of a family to her.

"What happened to Saaya?" I asked Daphne as I drove to the cafe, with her beside me, in Mitali's car.

"The last I saw her was at her engagement." She rambled. "She was absolutely fine, or maybe she pretended to be fine, or maybe she looked fine."

"Girls!" I stated. "Where is she now?"

"No idea. She doesn't get out much these days, after the breakup." Daphne replied. "Do you think something bad happened to Tim?"

"No. He should be fine." I pretended to have told the truth though I wasn't sure. I began to wonder about how much these people cared about him. Was a good friend that worth? If yes, was Tim that good a friend? How could he have been, as a person? How could he have people care so much about him?

Anil was waiting outside the cafe as we approached and he got into the rear seat of the car. "We're meeting Saaya's friend." He said giving me the directions. "Or do you want me to drive, Vian?"

"Nah that's fine. What kind of a guy was Tim?" I asked Anil, as I followed his directions.

"He's an asshole, man. Got into a lot of fights and befriended very few selected people in college, probably his own kind; rich." He alleged. "He was impolite, discourteous, and a spoilt brat."

"How can you be so sure?" I questioned him.

"After that encounter with Tim, we turned to our seniors to seek their help and they decided to have an interaction with him. Koster's rudeness aroused impatience and anger among the seniors and they got him to surrender by outnumbering him. Just to play a prank and frighten him, he was made to hold a bench between his jaws. He would bite the bench and they would hit him on the head with the textbooks." He detailed.

"Did he do it?" I asked, curious.

"No." he said. "He popped up a fight. One of the seniors gave him a few blows on the back of Tim's head with his palm, warning him to behave, and let him go."

"Koster just left? Without causing any trouble?" I asked surprised. I had already created in my mind an imaginary character of Tim Koster based on all that I had heard until then. It was hard to picture that character going down without a fight.

"For that instant, yes. But after college hours, Tim rammed into the senior's car with his, injuring him a little. They had a rash drive and clash of cars outside the college. So the other guy was injured, his car was damaged and his parents banned him from using a car." Anil finished.

"Whoa!" I exclaimed. "What about Tim?"

"He's filthy rich, man. He messes one car; he would get another. He had a way with the girls. He went around with about three girls from our college alone, excluding Saaya." He gave out. "One of them was my crush."

"Now I understand why he's your enemy." I commented.

"War and crime happens for two reasons, Vian! Money and women." He posited, looking away to his side, through the window.

"It took me a whole month to talk to that girl. She knew that he was trying to flatter her, so one day I was hanging out in the grounds with her and we noticed Koster approaching us." He went on.

""*Damn!*" I muttered to myself when I knew Tim was coming straight towards us.

"*Don't worry about it. I know how to deal with him.*" Asna assured me.

"*Hey!*" he greeted her as he came over and I only glared at him.

"*I'm not going to call you.*" Asna snapped before he could utter a word.

"*I know. That's why I'm going to call you today. I don't want it to sound like an anonymous call later today.*" He spoke surefooted and turned to leave.

"*What is your intention exactly?*" she questioned deviled by his attitude.

"*I like you. I would like to take you to dinner, and we can get to know each other.*" He smirked. "*Don't keep her long Anil. I got plans for her.*"

"*Son of a-*" I croaked, and made a move, with a sudden rage to hit him, but Asna stopped me.

"*Don't even bother. Ignore him.*""She said. I calmed down triumphantly at his failure to get my girl." Anil paused.

"So he failed?" I asked.

"No. She went away with him after college the next day and for few months after that until he got another girl." Daphne finished, laughing hard all of a sudden. All through that story, I was wondering why, Daphne was biting her lips. I failed to realize that she was trying her best not to laugh.

"He dumped her?" I was getting way curious than ever.

"He didn't. She said they were just good friends, but everyone says that she slept with him." Daphne said, looking at Anil through the rear view mirror. Anil, with a choleric expression on his face, pretended to ignore our conversation and I broke out into a heavy laugh.

"Come on man. It's not cool." He sounded ire.

"Ok. Sorry." I giggled and finally controlled myself while Daphne still found it hard not to laugh.

"That's her. That's Neeta." Anil called, pointing at a girl standing beside a moped. We pulled the car to beside her and asked her to get in. She was an average looking, traditionally dressed, average height and build but with a glow on her face. Anil made the formal introductions and he started shooting questions right away. "Did you talk to her?"

"Yes." She answered. "I wanted to tell her to go kiss her own back."

"Come on. She was your best friend." Daphne reminded.

"Not anymore. Not after she killed Tim Koster." Neetu expressed intense anger.

"What?" we snapped, Daphne and I.

"Yes. He met with an accident few days ago and died." She muttered.

"He died?" we screamed out of shock. "How do you know?" although I was sitting in the front seat, the part of body above my waist was twisted to the back.

"People are talking. No one could even see him after the accident." She said.

"He only went missing from the hospital. He didn't die." Daphne gave an outcry, gasping for breath. I let out a breath of relief too and turned to my front. I wasn't surprised the way people carry out certain news in chain. Add more story to the next guy who listens.

"Oh, thank God!" she exclaimed. "Everyone said he died and I thought it was true."

"No he's not." I corrected, with a cold grip of suspicion crawling down my neck. 'What if he really did die? What if no one has found him yet and he's lying down somewhere deserted? What if no one had managed to identify his body? Or is he just lying off in a cave waiting for his wounds to heal?'

"Well, at her engagement, I asked her to think again before doing it. *"There's nothing left to think anymore."* She sternly said. She was happy. She has the most glorious smile on her face. Probably because she was rid of Tim." She said.

"Does she know about the accident?" I asked.

"Yes." She replied. "I met her two days ago and told her that Tim Koster met with an accident. I didn't tell her he died because I was with a wrong idea that she couldn't take it if I broke it to her. *"I know."* She said. *"I heard about it."* She didn't have at least a slight frigging worried expression. She sounded as if she waited to hear that. *"Did you go to see him?"* I questioned her surprisingly. *"No."* she replied, looking

61

away. I asked why, and, *"There's nothing I can do to help him."* She spoke resentfully. Bloody witch"

"We thought Saaya would know something about him and hoped to find him with your help." I told her.

"Saaya is not bothered about him. She barricaded her mind from any news about Tim Koster." Neetu commented aggressively. "I never liked him until I saw the way he loved Saaya. I'll try to find something by tomorrow guys. I didn't know he went missing until you told me. Someone should know where he is. We just need to figure out whom to ask."

"Yes." Anil said.

"Hey I have to be heading somewhere." She said looking at her watch.

"Sure. We shall meet up some other time." Anil said as she reached for the door to get out.

"Sure. See you Daphne. It was nice meeting you Vian. See you." She bid farewell for the day.

"I still can't believe she did this to him." Anil commented. "He dug his own grave. He went crazy after her."

"How did they get together?" I asked,with an eagerness to know the story.

"Well, Saaya is not any ordinary girl. Her ethics were equally high along with her beauty. When Tim went after her, we were certain that she wouldn't fall for him. Apparently, somewhere deep within, we believed in Tim Koster's cunning tactics." He finished.

"I can see that she fell for him. I'm asking, how." I repeated.

"I don't know how. He had his own secretive ways of maneuver to flatter a girl." Anil praised. "Hunt him down and ask him yourself if you want the truth."

"I will." I played along with him and drove away.

"Where do I drop you off Daphne?" I asked, with my eyes fixed on the road ahead.

"Oh, I'm staying with Mitali tonight. I'm seeing her after a year and she's not keeping well." Daphne implied. We dropped off Anil at the café where he parked his bike and drove away.

"We shall check out Kosters' before we get back. Hope Tim's parents are back." I proposed, with curiosity hitting up inside me.

"Sure!"she agreed.

#4

I could say that though Daphne wasn't that close a friend to Tim, she very much hoped for him to be safe. The drive to Kosters' failed to meet our expectations of finding Tim's parents. The locks were still on the gates indicating that they hadn't returned yet. I drove back to Mitali's home in silence. "I can't believe this is happening." She said in a lowered tone. I didn't utter a word but drove. "Do you have a girlfriend?" she asked all of a sudden.

"I had." I answered in short.

"Where is she now?"

"Away." I answered blankly.

"What?" she snapped.

"She got married two days ago."

"Oh!" she sighed. "Why did you people breakup?"

"I didn't."

"Hmm. Why did she breakup?" she shot another questioned, being childish, thinking for less than five seconds after every answer I gave to her question. I gave her the name of the musician whom Tianna married.

"Oh, I get it." She murmured to herself. "Listen. The next time a girl tells you that she loves you, marry her the next minute, and then tell her that you love her too."

"That's very thoughtful of you." I japed, making a funny face at her.

"Oh come on. At least you were not a coward who wouldn't stand up for her." She tried to pep up my mood, pulling me out of my gloomy past.

Mitali was seated on the spiral staircase at the side of the house, as we drove in through the gate. She was waiting for us, I could tell by the look of anxiety on her face, with traces of tautness. Her face looked worn off due to lack of proper rest. "What do you have?" she asked, in a weakened lowered tone, pulling herself up and leaning forward on the handrails.

"Nothing. We met Neeta. She'll get us something tomorrow." I said. I ascended a few steps to her and sat down one step above her. Her fever went down but she needed rest. I told her what we learnt from Neeta. I failed to come to a conclusion about Saaya without knowing the whole story. Besides, I didn't hold any right to come to a conclusion about her. Daphne and I tried to distract Mitali's mind from Tim Koster, so as to make her rest her illness. Daphne was good at cheering her up. We chit chatted for a little while and I started to yawn. I decided to crash the bed and walked away inside. I overslept the next morning and Daphne woke me up,

"Neeta called. She'd meet us in an hour. Get ready." She said and left the room, pulling away the blanket in which I was covered. Smiling to her cunning way of teasing, I got up from the bed lazily and walked into the bathroom. I stood under the shower, thinking of any possibility of finding Tim Koster. Mitali couldn't come with us until she recovered completely. Daphne and I took off after a light breakfast to meet Anil and Neeta.

"Where shall we go?" Anil asked, as he got in with Neeta.

"Tell me about his lifestyle. What he liked. Where he went the most." I asked.

"He goes to gym. He does a lot of boxing." Anil said without a thought. "His car! He gets his car done by a mechanic. Any repair or vinyl's or water wash, whatever."

We drove to a boxing club in Parsi Colony in East Mumbai, as we spoke. "Saaya knows nothing. Even if she knew something, she wouldn't tell. She wouldn't even talk about him." Neeta started to complain.

"Can we get his parents' phone numbers or something?" I asked, as I drove.

"I tried calling to his mom's number, but it was switched off." Neeta said. "I'm afraid that something bad could have happened to him."

"Bad in the sense what?" Daphne gave her a strange look.

"Bad as in he died."

"Come on." Anil cut her off.

"What! I called like twenty people since yesterday evening. Everyone says he died." Neeta contended.

"No one saw his body, or attended his funeral, did they?" Anil continued, "How come I haven't heard about any of this?"

"Why would anyone bother telling you this? You were enemies with him." Daphne stated.

We reached the boxing club and I drove into the parking. "You girls stay here." I ordered as Anil and I got out of the car." We walked straight into the club and took a quick look around. I took a few more steps inside and,

"Can I help you?" a man in early thirties walked towards us, wiping the sweat off his face with a napkin.

"Yes, Vian!" I introduced myself shoving my hand for a shake. Taking it,

"Coach!" he replied. "What can I do for you?"

"We're friends with Tim Koster." Anil gave in. "When was the last time he had been around?"

"About two weeks ago I should say. Why do you ask?" Coach questioned.

"He went missing one and a half week ago. We have been searching for him." Anil went on.

"What happened to him?"

"He met with an accident later and went missing from the hospital." Anil said.

The coach bore, all of a sudden, the same dreaded expression I had been seeing since I started to hear about Tim Koster. "Missing?"

"Yes." I sternly replied. "We were hoping to find a clue to pick something to him."

"He used to come in regularly and stay late, punching the bags aggressively; very aggressively." The coach started. "He never talked, his last few days here. All he did was, punch the bags and plant his frustration onto them through his fists."

"Did he share anything with you or anyone close to him in here?" I asked.

"He never made friends with anyone here. He followed a reserved path." The coach assured. "The only sound we heard from him was the sound of pounding of his fists on the bags. I overheard his conversation with his girlfriend and figured that he was having a breakup."

"Let us know if you hear about him." Anil told him, handing a card to him.

The coach didn't utter a word but stare at the card, with a shocked feeling covering his face. We walked out of the club and to the car, disappointed, that we couldn't find a clue. "You know what, Anil? Saaya is such a monster." Neeta muttered, with clenched teeth.

"What's wrong?" he questioned.

"She just called Saaya to ask if she heard something."

Daphne gave in.

"" I'm more concerned about my fiancée than Tim Koster. I don't even care if he's dead." That was her answer." Neeta interrupted.

Anil and I got into the car and sat there without a word. "What's wrong with her?" he broke into choler.

"Tim fell in love with a hoe." Neeta stated. I shifted up the gear and drove away in silence with wrath, but failed to join them in accusing Saaya. All that started to develop a compulsive spirit in me, empowered by curiosity and anxiety about Tim Koster's story. I was eager to propel myself to inquire and remove the cover over Tim Koster and Saaya Viroodh's story. "Saaya is trying to make Tim's death an inevitable event."

"At some point of her life, she'll regret it." Daphne swore.

Neeta sat behind darting storming glares out through the window. We spent the day roaming around, trying to pick up hints or evidence which might help us find Tim Koster.

"Anything?" Mitali asked eagerly as I walked in through the door in the evening.

"Yes. We found out what a demon Saaya could be." Daphne said in a lowered tone, trying to be careful so that Mitali's parents wouldn't hear her.

"What happened?" she asked horrendously at Daphne's reaction. I narrated to her all that we found out that day, and Mitali stood aghast, her jaw dropping every moment. "Write Koster's story and get it out, Vian."

"I was thinking the same." I blurted out.

"What?" Daphne snapped.

"You heard me." I said. "I want this story to be told."

Daphne and Mitali stared at me with dismayed look on their faces. "You sure?"

"I wasn't sure until today. I have a feeling that there is much more to him we can imagine. There shouldn't be left any stones unturned."

"I'm with you." Daphne agreed.

I decided to inform Uncle Jamie about it once I made a draft of the story or at least a few sample chapters. "Tell you what! That's a good idea. I don't want his death to go wasted." Mitali accorded with us.

"Don't you guys think that you're exaggerating? When you finally meet him again, it could probably be like everything had been totally fine and you just managed to stress your brains out with your over thinking.

"Mission Tim Koster then." Daphne joked. We changed the subject as we saw Mitali's dad walk to us.

"How was the day?" he asked.

"Pretty good." I said.

Say no to heartbreaks

#5

My eagerness to investigate on Tim Koster and Saaya's story deprived me of my sleep that night. I had an extreme urge to dwell in his story to get the facts straight. I wondered, despite all the hearsay information, if Tim Koster was still alive. I wondered if I could get a chance to meet Tim Koster somehow, but I knew I had to bring forth his story beyond the rumors that were floating around. It would be necessary for me to make many friends to get the story. I would have had to go through many trifles and cross hurdles, to know the truth. I would have had to undergo restlessness to work on Tim Koster's story. I sent an email to Uncle Jamie asking him for a month's time to get him a good story. All I needed to do was to find Kosters and interact with them to get the permission to write about their son and convincing Saaya Viroodh was going to be arduous task as well. I didn't know how I was going to accomplish the task, but I was compulsive to do it no matter what. After all, with hard work, comes success. I dozed off to sleep after midnight and woke up after a short early morning nap. The morning was too dark and the sun kept me waiting. I leaned onto the wall by the head of the bed, with my laptop in the biting cold, to start writing the story. I could hear distant sounds of steel vessels in the kitchen and a little while later, Mitali's mom walked into the bedroom with a mug of coffee.

"You up so early?" she asked as she placed the coffee mug on the table. "Not sleepy?"

"Couldn't find enough sleep. Thank you." I said as I took the mug into my hand. As I opened the blank document, Tianna's memories began to haunt my mind. I couldn't find the strength to cope up with recurring nightmares of her. Her voice stomping heavily inside my head, I hit the keys on my laptop vigorously, but it went vain and I ended up erasing every word I had typed. The sunrise broke my zeal to write and I got up from the bed. I took an early morning shower and walked out to find Mitali listening to songs in her mobile, seated at the staircase.

"Good morning." She tweeted as I sat beside her. "I'm coming with you guys today."

"What was Tim Koster like?" I asked her.

She looked up as she thought and twirled her lips together. "He was often misunderstood by everyone. He was arrogant, but he was kind. He got into a lot fights, but also made a lot of good friends. He never did hurt a girl. I, like everybody else flinched at the sound of his name in the beginning. He always had a fierce look on his face. His arguments were ferocious and savage. His first passing by affair in college was with Gargi and I developed a disgusted feeling towards him. But then, there was this guy, Nevan from our class who paid his college fee from his part time job. Anil's friend crashed into Nevan's bike with his car accidentally, but blamed Nevan for parking it wrong. When Nevan was surrounded by seniors, Tim came forward to help him and stood up for him.

73

"" *Do you know how much it's going to cost us?*" they started.

"*You sure as hell have no idea either since your dad probably bought it for you.*" Tim interrupted the guy who owned the car. "*Let him be.*"

"*Stay out of this.*" They warned Tim.

"*It's not his fault. Let him go and get his bike fixed.*" Tim argued.

"*Or what?*" they pushed onto him.

"*Its gon' be another car today.*" Tim raised his voice, taking his place beside Nevan, and they started to back off. "*Now pay for his bike.*"

"*He'll get it fixed.*" Anil compromised the situation. I thought that he wasn't that bad after all." Mitali finished.

I listened to her quietly as Daphne joined us with drowsy eyes, yawning. "What's the plan today?" she asked as she sat in my front.

"I want to meet Asna and Gargi." I proposed.

"Anil won't come with us to meet Asna." She reminded.

"We shall meet him after Asna leaves then." I said. Mitali's mom called us in for breakfast and Daphne went to freshen up. Mr. Rao couldn't digest that Tim Koster was no more. I tried to convince them that he might have been alive somewhere but India is a country that lives off rumors and untrue gossips. I wasn't sure about his survival myself. However, everyone believed Tim Koster to be dead and that his parents disappeared to bury him in secrecy away from the wicked world which had cost his life. It was more like they were framing the story for me to write.

Daphne arranged a meeting with Asna and convinced her to talk to me in private about Tim Koster. She was beautiful, and the sign of her beauty consecrated Tim Koster's taste. She gave me a good impression on Tim and without wasting any time, I asked her straight away, as we sat in the café coffee day,

"What happened the evening after you met Anil at the college grounds?"

"Well, Tim always asked me out but I was afraid of him. That evening when he called, I answered his call with a feeling of intense anger. I was going to shout at him. Nevertheless, his voice was so soft and smoothening. It carried an ice cold feeling to which I was flattered. His words were convincing and I agreed to have dinner with him. He came with a flower bouquet and treated me with a decent behavior. He didn't flirt but made me laugh until my stomach ached. I mistook him to be a rough kind earlier but then I realized that I was wrong about him. I ended up enjoying his company." She went on. "We got close but he warned me not to take the relation any farther and I was ok with it. He was just a guy who wanted to make friends. No bullshit."

"You mean?"

"We were in a really good relationship; just two people without chemistry. Like two guy friends hang out together, fool around together. He broke away from Gargi who happened to be a slut. She was having a passing by affair with one of our seniors and Tim broke up with her when he found out about it. She promised him that she'd stop seeing that senior guy, but Tim wouldn't give in. That was how Gargi and I became enemies at college. She accused me of stealing Tim from her." She finished.

"I believe he must have told you about Gargi. What's her story?" I questioned.

"Gargi used to flirt with him in class. I was new to college back then and didn't mingle much with anyone. She showed towards him, possessiveness and genitive caring. She fought with him every time he spoke to some other girl or likewise. Everyone knew that she was hitting on him and everyone knew why. He was filthy rich and wouldn't get into serious relationships. Gargi's parents were too strict and hence she always played safe. To hint him of her intentions and feelings on him, she went over to his place one Sunday and romanced with him without actually proposing to him. To let him know that she was only attracted to him and it wasn't going to end as a married relation; and Tim played along with her. But he thought he was the only one she was attracted to. He didn't at first realize that she was attracted to almost every guy who had hit on her." Asna inveighed against Gargi. "After all her bitching on him, she made it look like he played her. Only the people whom she played knew what had actually happened."

"How did you guys get along?" I asked, paying keen interest on her story.

"We got along very well. He tried not to get into trouble with Anil, but seniors were stridently furious at Tim for every reason. They always picked on chances to get back at him but Tim was impossible. He wasn't strong enough for all of them but everyone was afraid of what he could do later." Asna spoke in extolment. "He made me live with self-respect and independently. Above all, he taught me how to live a life of fun."

I stopped asking her further questions when she started to breakdown into a cry. "He was very special to me. He had a beautiful life. If only she hadn't messed it up." She sobbed.

"It's alright. We don't know what exactly happened between them, do we?" I consoled her, pushing her cup of coffee closer to her and she took it up. I tried to distract her off all of it for a while but she was already a strong girl who knows how to hide her feelings.

#6

The next day, Mitali, Daphne and I had lunch in a restaurant talking about our next plans and else after vacation. We only had two weeks left to return back to New York. Post lunch at around half past three, Anil insisted that he'd come along with us to meet Gargi, 'cause he was sure she'd lose her tongue on Asna if he wasn't there with us. We met her at the beach later that evening. She looked like any regular girl. Not too traditional and not too modern. She bore an innocent look on her face which raised a slight doubt as to why, since it didn't look natural.

"Hey!" she exclaimed as she saw Mitali, Daphne, Anil and me. "How are you Mitali? I miss you so much. How long are you going to stay?" and she hugged both Mitali and Daphne.

"I'll stick around for a week or two."Mitali forced a smile.

I wondered if Gargi really loved her or if she was just pretending to be so nice to her in the face. Or maybe it's just the way girls greet each other, with a lot of excitement kicking out from deep inside. However, when we asked about Tim, she refused to tell us anything. I requested her that it was important but she looked at us with disdain. Anil, Daphne, Mitali and just waited for her to start talking as she sat beside Daphne while the rest of us stood in front of her with patience.

"I loved him. I wanted to share my life with him." She started. We were struck with dumbfound feelings on hearing her first statement. Daphne rolled her eyes and Mitali put up a disgusted look, as Gargi stared down at the ground. Anil controlled himself from laughing out on the other hand. "I was very friendly with him and when he proposed to me, I was shocked. I didn't expect he'd mistake my intimacy towards himfor love. But I gave it a thought for a few days and felt warmth in his love. I loved him back. I got addicted to talking over the phone with him. I went nuts to look into his eyes every time I met him. I loved the way he reacted to my surprises. Many other guys were into me but I rejected them all for him. I felt that he was the one for me. We were very happy, until Asna stole him from me. She stole him from my world. I still love him and can't accept anybody else." She pretended to cry.

I gestured Anil to stop, when I noticed that he was going to defend Asna. He put a serious look on his face and turned away biting the inside of his lips. "Is this exactly what happened between Tim Koster and you?" I asked, blankly looking at her fake saddened face.

"Yes." She replied, shedding a tear with a great effort.

"Sean's gonna be here in few minutes." Anil told Daphne, pretending to read a message on his mobile. Gargi rushed as she heard that and hastily took up her handbag which was lying beside her.

"I gotta go." She said.

"How did Koster propose to you?" Daphne questioned her.

"He- uh- over the phone. He proposed to me over the phone." Gargi stammered.

"When was that?" Daphne shot her another question and I only stood there staring at her as an upset tensed look crept all over her face.

"I don't remember." She uttered in a lowered voice.

"How could you not remember the date Koster proposed to you when you truly loved him?" Daphne asked again.

"It was a random evening and we were having a casual conversation over the phone." She lied. "I gotta go. I just got reminded of an important work I had to finish."

"Wait until Sean comes." Anil stressed.

"No, really. I'll catch up some other time. I don't know him so well anyway." She went on, getting up on her feet and pulling out her car keys out of the handbag. "It was a pleasure meeting you, Vian. We shall catch up some other time." I saw her hop into her red hatchback car and drive away.

"Who's Sean?" I asked Anil, turning back to him.

"Her past and present boyfriend." Mitali answered. "Anil's batch mate and our senior. Poor guy loves her really bad. She dumped him when she found Koster. She was with few other guys but always kept Sean in the loop. People say that she's now out of her games and is being nice to Sean but he doesn't know the whole truth yet. What a slut! She was all over Koster and everyone knows it. She was seeing Sean too, while she was in relation with Koster. No wonder people call her a hoe."

"Come on, now. Let's get out of it for a while." I tried to divert their minds. We had some ice creams and fun before we started back home.

"We shall meet Sean if possible and see what he might say." Anil suggested while getting down the car at coffee day. "Say tomorrow?"

"That would be great." I complimented.

Something was waiting for Mitali as I drove through the gate and parked the car. She burst out of the car kicking open the door, overwhelmed at the sight of Ryna and his parents walk out through the door; but she held back her excitement, going diffidently shy all of a sudden. Ryna's father let out an adorable smile at her and patted her head gently. Ryna introduced me to his dad and we walked in together. Daphne stuck with me timidly as Mitali was busy with Ryna's family.

"What's going on?" Daphne asked me in a whisper, with her sparkling eyes, looking around at them all. The living room was filled with chatter and scent of delicious food. Mrs. Rao handed two bowls of sweet, each one to Daphne and me and rushed into the kitchen.

Before I could think of an answer for her, "We shall arrange the engagement sometime next week and after they finish up with their education, we shall get them married." Ryna's father broke the news. Both their faces turned iridescent at the sweet news and Mitali looked at Ryna with a demure expression on her face. Mitali and Ryna's parents got busy with the planning and Ryna turned serious all of a sudden making sure no one was noticing him.

"Did you find anything?" he asked, looking at Daphne, Mitali and me, one after the other.

"Not much." I sighed. My confidence was left troubled, with a sudden fear that Tim Koster might have been dead and that all his friends would be devastated. I wished that if it were a mere rumor, I could travel and transform myself to where it was originated from, and prevent it from spreading like a wildfire. "Koster's house is locked." I reported. "No one knows where else they could be."

My mind toiled to dig something out from Gargi's twaddle story, from Asna's veracity about him. Devise to resolve the puzzle tumbled out of my reach. I felt like my neural system started to conk out. The gathering was relishing and savory but I remained bewildered. The evening was embroiled into perplexed convulsion. That night, I crept into a deep sleep until the sunrays hit my face with warmth the next morning.

Mitali's house became very fussy for the next few days, with the preparations for the engagement. I averted myself from Tim Koster's case, to conceal the fray, to not to mess up the engagement. I have never seen Mitali so happy. She moved around in the house jocund and merrily. She almost washed out Mr. Rao's bank account with her shopping episode. Ryna bought her some presents as well and a beautiful dress. We hired a very good photographer for the event, for Mitali was fond of photographs. She spent most of her time posing for the photos than greeting guests and relatives. Mr. Rao's face was cleared of signs of dubiety about Mitali and Ryna. He looked extremely happy that Mitali and Ryna were getting engaged and he wouldn't have to worry about anything anymore.

Mom and dad started calling me everyday, asking me to come back so that they could spend time with me before they returned to India. Or else I would have had to wait a while for them to return to India and stick with them for a week or two.Tianna's memories haunted me every minute, creeping into my head no matter how hard I tried to ignore. My tensions brewed as I thought more about her. I tried hard to snub what she had done, but it didn't help. I would shake my head vigorously and pull myself back into my world from the valley of her memories. I would go for a drive alone while everyone else was busy, to check if Kosters were back. I was never surprised, to see the same locks to the gates. Mitali and Ryna's faces carried joyful expressions which acted as layers to conceal their hostilities. They struggled hard to force smiles when everybody moved on thinking that Tim Koster was dead. Mrs. Rao asked Mitali if she'd invite Saaya for the engagement, unaware of the recent events until Tim Koster went missing, to dead.

"I'd rather invite my enemies over if I had." She scoffed.

"What happened between you two now?" Mrs. Rao questioned, in a whisper, so that the relatives wouldn't catch her puzzled voice.

"Girlish matters, aunty." Ryna covered it up to prevent unnecessary attention. Mrs. Rao didn't know much as Mr. Rao, about Tim Koster. Ryna and Mitali's engagement went great like the celebration of a festival. My best friends were beautiful and handsome. I wished everyday was their engagement day, so they would remain so happy their entire lives. I could listen to the song of their life. I could imagine how happy they were going to be together. I could feel the triumphant success of their love. I could see the victory in their exchanging smiles. I could feel the pride they carried in their eyes. I could envisage the pain and sorrow they were going to kiss goodbye. Tianna's breaking apart from me hurt me so bad at the sight of Ryna and Mitali's unify. My heart started to beat rapidly. It could have been the same with us if she hadn't broken up.

The following day was just another day. All that I was left to be was what I had to pretend to be. I feigned that I was happy and over Tianna. But deep inside, I was bound to see the tears I cried. I fought them behind my eyes to send them back down and overlaid incomplete smiles and muted laughter. I was afraid that I would have had to wet my eyes when I laughed. "How's your novel going?" Ryna asked a few days after the engagement, as we drove to meet Sean. "Coming good?"

"Yeah." I answered, forcing a smile, bringing myself back from Tianna's world. 'She was married and it was wrong for me to think about her.' I thought. "It's coming good." I kept blinking my eyesto ease them from the burning sensation they had, from the overnight cry.

"What's wrong?" Ryna asked as he drove and I sat behind Mitali and him with Daphne.

"Nothing." I lied. "Couldn't get enough sleep."

I kind of underestimated them both. "Get over her, Vian." Mitali said. "Move on and be happy. Get back to yourself. You don't have to cry over a girl like her. She didn't deserve you in the first place. Work on your novel. Deviate yourself with it."

I only remained seated with silence, looking out of the window. Daphne stared at me helplessly, unaware of what to talk. "I'm trying." I said.

"No." Ryna snapped. "Don't get over her yet. Continue thinking about her. Hurt your feelings with her memories." He glanced at me through the mirror and turned back to the road.

"Stop joking, Ryna." Mitali scoffed and Daphne looked at him puzzled. I persisted in hiding my face from them, in case I broke down into a cry.

"Do I look like I'm joking?" he asked back in an irritated voice. "Seriously Vian. Continue to be what you are now. Continue to feel the hurt. Use every chance to think about her. Love her. Cry if you have to that she ditched you because she was a coward to stay strong with you. Do not use your writing. You understand me? Do not take the help of your novel to forget her. Use your aggression on your writing. Be violent. Use the sorrow past with her, in shaping your novel well. Write it with all the sadness you've got to bring out the pleasant soothing music in it. Lead astray all the people who are as hurt and broken as you are, with your writing."

#7

He was right in every way. I wanted the pain to be told and heard. I hankered to dig in deep into Tim Koster's life and make his pain and suffering to echo. I wanted everyone to cognize or better yet, realize how bad a person could be hurt. 'Love is not just an ache in the head. It's not a mere part in a body. It's interlinked with the soul, and the damage it does can never be healed.' I thought. I wanted the lament song of Tim Koster to be heard. I wanted people to realize that they were bored of success stories. I wanted them to know how strong they needed to stand when someone tried to break them. I wanted them to know that listening to Eminem when low was not the only solace.

Sean arrived at Juhu beach ten minutes before we did. Anil was waiting too by the time we reached. Formal introductions were made and Sean congratulated Mitali and Ryna for being engaged. "So you guys met Gargi yesterday?" he asked.

"Yeah. She didn't tell you?" Daphne asked.

"When was she honest with me?" he scoffed. Anil let out a short grin. "I'm sorry about Koster. He was a good guy."

"Was Gargi in serious love with Koster?" I questioned.

"Ask her what love is, and she'll look it up in a dictionary." He mocked, which made Daphne and Mitali break into a heavy laugh.

"She told us that her love towards Koster was true." I said.

"You can call that fantasy." He mocked again.

"She's in a relation with you now, isn't she?" I asked.

"For now, yes."

"So what do you think about her?"

"I'm not sure how long she's going to stay with me."

"Come on, Sean!" Daphne hit his shoulder and he laughed away. "Why wouldn't you break up with her then?"

"I fell in love with her. I found out the strumpet in her but it was too late. I was terribly in love with her. She tends to go low at times and I'm the only one she turns to. I just can't see her cry but I'm starting to tire of her games. She turned to be unbearable. As of now she promised me she'd change and stay true to me, but I'm not sure if I can trust her." He finished.

"How did you- er- how did you guys?" I stammered. "I don't know how to put this."

"It's alright, I got it." He said. "I was just a normal friend to her and one day, some guy dumped her. She said that it was her third relation and cried horribly that she was ditched. I consoled her and cared for her. I helped her move on and helped her realize how precious she was. I talked her out of all her pain. I used to take her out whenever she felt lonely. I talked her to sleep every night and made sure she'd find my "good morning" messages every morning after she woke up. She proposed to me after a few days and it was very quick. I talked it out with her and construed that she was indeed in love with me and cared for me. I smiled to her voice, I bent my head down for her when she kissed me, I filled my hands with the touch of her palms, and I breathed her essence. She took out all the bitter in my life and sweetened it. Things turned sour eventually." He paused, losing himself into unknown recollection.

"Things like what?" I questioned.

"I realized that for her, being in love means tightening things up between us. I felt like I was incarcerated. She confined me to a lot of restrictions and accused me of romancing and flirting with other girls. To her, being in love, means checking my mobile for anyconversationwith girls while she wouldn't let me touch hers. She always had a lock to her message folder. I somehow found that she was flirting with other guys. "*You don't trust me, do you?*" she screamed at me whenever I questioned her. "*How could you lose faith in me? How could you do that to me?*" I knew what the truth was, but I had to stay shut to calm her down. And there comes Tim Koster." He paused and looked at me. I had my eyes fixed on him with a greed for the truth in the story.

"Tim Koster was a very friendly guy. He would wait

to know and understand someone before he reacted. If you're nice to him, he'll be nice to you no matter who you are. He won't give a damn if you stick your leg on his path for him to tumble. That's the reason these guys had trouble with him. He made pretty good friends in class. He was smart, kind, and knew how to deal with every dork and ally. Rich and poor didn't bother him much. He was neutral to weak and strong. Gargi used to talk to me a lot about him. I empathized that she was into him and obsessed with him. I was afraid that if Tim Koster hits on her, she'd definitely accept to him, but I realized that I was so wrong about her." He went on, until Daphne interrupted him,

"What?" she asked.

"Yes. She was the one who started hitting him." Sean sounded like it was a joke.

"Oh!" Daphne exclaimed. "How did that happen?"

"Well one night over the phone, *"Tim asked me if I had a boyfriend."* She said.

"Oh! What did you say?" I asked.

"I said that I was single." She continued. *"It's not about you. I wanted to tell him proudly that I was with you, but I wanted to see if he was interested in me."*

"Why would you want to know if he's interested in you when you're with me?" I asked with disappointment and sudden fear dashing down my gut.

"I just want to know." She answered irritatingly.

"What would you do if he's interested in you?" I asked.

"I don't know. I'm with you, right? What could I do?" she answered in a reckless manner. She fell asleep after a while but I stayed up all night worried about what was wrong with her. Day after day, it grew harder to get a hold of her. She exchanged phone numbers with Tim one day. She called me that night with an annoying tone.

"Hello?" I answered, and,

"He's not answering my calls." She complained with a scream.

"Who?" I questioned.

"Tim Koster!"

"What's the matter?"

"Just like that?" I gibed and remained silent. I wondered what she was up to. *"He's not answering."*

"Why are you so bothered?" I sternly questioned.

"I feel awkward when somebody doesn't respond to me." She went on.I continued my silence and she understood that I was riling. She came back to her senses then and started talking normally. It didn't end there. It turned her into some sort of madness for Koster. He firmly kept to himself but she went bugging him. She spent her time with me, but kept sending him texts or chatting with him. I don't know what charm she bestowed upon him, but he lost it and flirted back with her.She started to avoid me. She tried to forefend our relation saying she tried to be with me but couldn't. She ended it up so easily saying we could have been good friends. I was partly thankful to Koster that he took her away from me and gave me freedom to have a life with my friends again. At the same time, I was shattered, because I loved her.

Anyway, there was nothing I could do. I couldn't force her to come back. I couldn't keep her chained with me. The only choice I had was to let her go. Everybody began to blabber about their relation. About how deep, Gargi was into him and everybody wondered how long she was going to stay with him. She was lucky that she didn't get a chance to ditch Koster, because Koster's paybacks could be so detestable and deplorable. He had all the fun he could have with her for a while, and somehow, Anil caught his eye." Sean joked and giggled at Anil. "Asna wasn't that clean but she definitely isn't that bad either. She was sweet and made sure she hurt no one. Let's not talk about her. I don't have the right." He finished.

"How did he end up with Asna? Didn't Gargi object?" I questioned.

"Well, Gargi kept me in the loop all the while. Spoke sweet with me incase she needed me anytime. Koster wasn't blind. When Gargi found out he was seeing Asna, Gargi created a scene that he was the one who was after her, and then he cheated her. Tim Koster patiently listened to all her racket with few others in his class, and walked over to the center, then placed his mobile on an empty bench. *There is a reason why I don't clear my inbox. Everybody's free to go through including you, and I will go through yours. If I so much as find that you don't have a single message of flirt in your phone with any other guy apart from me, during the span of our relation, I WILL MARRY YOU.*" He stated.

"*You don't trust me, do you?*" she popped her usual drama.

"*No I don't.*" he said out without a second thought and she gasped with a mixed feeling of puzzle and fearful guilt. "*I don't trust you a single bit.*" She stared at the rest of the class, and his mobile, and turned away to leave. *"Sure you wanna leave? I gave you a chance to prove that I hold the blame."*

She didn't listen to him. She didn't bother turning back. She just kept walking until she was out of their sight. She kept walking until she found another fool. "Who's that?" Mitali questioned.

"Me." He answered, stunningly and we broke into a laugh.

"What did you do?" Ryna asked.

"What else do we do when we see a girl cry? Especially when she's the one we love. We look through the darkness in her and try to brighten her up." He said. "I did the same. I forgave her, the moment she shed tears on my shoulders."

"Yeah, the cry drama. Pfft!" Anil barbed, shaking his head.

He went along with Asna very well. They were cool with each other. No one had the nerve to point them out, but then after one year, Saaya Viroodh joined our college. She was Koster's junior. I don't know the exact story since I was busy baring and handling Gargi's insanity. Maybe she's changed now, but I can't trust her. My father discords my relation with her and I gave her a hint that I might have to let her go. She accused my family of being unworthy that they couldn't have her. She woke up the following day with a misapprehension that a simple apology would make me forget what she spoke about my family. I would never accept a girl who disrespects my family. It all depends on her now, on how she's going to sort this out.

#8

'People could be so weird.' I thought as we drove towards Kosters' that evening before we had to start to the airport to travel to New York. 'Rolling back to the previous centuries, Indian culture was sacred. Marriages were made in heaven. Parents were considered Gods. Houses were felt as homes. Relations and sentiments were dainty. Helping hands existed abundantly. People visited temples, mosques and churches for pleasant minds. Hearts had room for everyone. Favors and gratitude were exchanged. Self-respect and dignity were regarded as the only riches. Love and relationships persisted eternally. But forward in time, everything roughened the acculturation. Marriages are made in a hurry. Parents are considered mere mentors. Houses are considered shelters. Relations and sentiments became immure. Helping hands decayed. People visit temples, mosques and churches to pray for their selfish greed. Hearts have room for things. Favors are done with expectations. Self-respect and dignity are just characteristic features. Love and relationships are fun. Loyalty comes with a price.'

Ryna pulled the car to a halt in front of the gate to

Kosters' and drove away disappointed at the locks still on them. I took a short glance and fell back into my thoughts.

"Ryna?" Mitali called, her eyes fixed onto a car that was approaching us from the opposite side and then drove past us.

"Kosters." Ryna gasped and steered the wheel taking a U turn. He drove back to the house where the Kosters' driver was unlocking the gate. I couldn't look through the tinted glass.

"Uncle?" Mitali and Ryna hurried up to their car as Daphne and I got down and waited by the car since it wouldn't have looked if all of us barged onto their car.

"We can't talk right now, Ryna. I suggest you let this go." He spoke as he lowered down the window.

"Where is he?"

"We have no idea. We're trying to find out." He replied sternly. "I would really appreciate if you kids can let us be." The driver got back in the car and drove away into the house through the massive gates. Ryna and Mitali exchanged shocked expressions and walked back to us disappointed.

Daphne promised us that she'd try talking to Kosters and find something out as Mr. Rao hurried us to the airport.We bid farewell before the check-in and walked away disappointed. Mitali's eyes were covered in tears as we left due to the departing from her parents and Tim Koster's agony. We sat in extreme silence in the plane throughout the journey. Mom and dad waited for us with a contrived setting for dinner at Uncle Silburn's place. We freshened up and climbed downstairs eager to see what they were up to. Tony was seated at the dinner table, his eyes shining brightly. We figured that there was some upgrade with Lisa. We were equally surprised to see him so happy.

"Don't tell us that you're married to her." Ryna joked as he walked to him and Tony got up from the chair to give him a tight hug.

"I'm gonna propose to her tomorrow." He blurted out as he broke free from Ryna's hug.

"Holy crap, you serious?" I shouted, with excitement running up my neck, and flung myself onto him.

My parents and Uncle Silburn were curious to know about Tim Koster. After patiently listening to all the events, they couldn't utter a word either. Uncle Silburn supported me to take longer if needed to get the story good. Dad showed utmost interest with my story. He suggested me to schedule a travel to India after we complete our exams. Ryna and Mitali would be getting married after the exams. Uncle Silburn went through all the drafts of my findings about the story of Tim Koster and he was pretty impressed.

"I still can't place it in front of the board, unless you complete it with a proper interesting entry." He said.

"I'll get it." I said confidently. "All I need is time."

"You have it, but you better hurry." He warned.

#9

Tony was all set for his proposal. He was positive that Lisa would be thrilled. From what he told us, they have been hanging out lately and shared an intimate relation. She would utilize every chance she could have to spend time with him and seemed very happy. Tony longed for her to have that very joyousness, throughout her life. He could barely sleep. We could see the excitement kicking up inside him. He left a greeting in one of her books which she would open the next day in class. Everything went according to his plan. Lisa met him on his way to class from the parking and we walked in together.I could smell delight from Tony's anxiousness. Lisa pulled out her books but didn't open any of them. Tony began to tap his feet, with tension drawing in his veins. Lisa turned back with a bewildered face and Tony suddenly changed his worried expression to casual look. Lisa continued to stare at him. "She saw the card, dude." Ryna muttered, with his lips closed. Tony observed her for a few seconds and nodded to her asking what was wrong. She nodded back a nothing and turned back to her front. Pausing for a few seconds, she took a scrupulous look around at the class. Everyone seemed to be busy with their own work. She bore a baffled look for the rest of the sessions. Tony prepped himself for the surprise. He thought over and over again, trying to figure out if it was the best way or not. He had a tough time changing expressions every time Lisa turned back to look at him, to see if he was the one who put the card. "Come on, man. It's gonna go good. Stop worrying about it." Ryna tried to comfort him.

"I don't know. I don't know man." Tony stuttered. "You of all people should try to understand, that this is a moment where people get on tenterhooks worse than waiting for a death sentence."

"Did you go through my books yesterday evening?" Lisa whispered during the break, bending over to Tony's ear.

"Your books? Why would I?" Tony continued to stammer. "No." he then answered grimly. "Anything wrong?"

She walked away, ignoring his question pretending that nothing was wrong, and her face depicting disappointment. I wondered, worried and was afraid if they were going to be fine. I then realized that love had never been ended in this world.

"College dance hall, 5 30 PM." Tony left a note stuck to Lisa's locker and ran back to join us before she came. She picked it out as we walked towards her, watching. Tony, barging his way through us from the back, approached her, pretending to be cool,

"Hey! We're going to a movie tonight. You wanna come along?" he asked, ignoring the note in her hands. She looked into his eye to know if he was the one who put the note and, "What's the matter?" he asked, taking the note from her hands. He took a quick look and going dull in face all of a sudden, "Oh! Ok." He sighed. "See you tomorrow, then."

Tony walked away dissatisfied, with Lisa watching him leave with horrified look on her face. She looked back at the note, and "See you tomorrow." Ryna patted her head as we left. We met Mitali outside and she broke into a heavy laugh as we told her of Tony's acting.

"What if she doesn't turn up?" Mitali asked him.

"She will." Tony blushed.

We hurried to the dance hall and reached by five past five, to ensure everything was arranged according to the plan."Son of a-" Ryna exclaimed as he saw the arrangements that have been made. "When did you-?" We stood there aghast, astonished by the setting. Tony arranged a DJ and lighting effects with colorful decorations in the dance hall.

Tony's movements were rapid and nervous. He repeated everything he spoke. Lisa would walk in any minute then. "Calm down, alright? Everything's cool." The DJ assured him, with his hand over Tony's shoulder.A friend of Tony's called up to his cell and informed him of Lisa's arrival. Everybody took their places and the lights were hit out. She barged in through the door, with infuriating anger and searched in the darkness of the hall. A spotlight was focused onto her with a beaming sound. The exasperating look on her face was as clear as crystal in the focus light. The DJ started playing sudden romantic music which broke the silence in the dance hall. Lisa started to scream something out which was deafened by the music in the hall. There was a beautiful dance of the lights on the walls of the hall, framing symbols and letters. It was pitch dark except for the lighting Terpsichore and focus light on Lisa. The words "WILL YOU MARRY ME?" were displayed with the lighting in the midair, along with the music, as Lisa continued to show her foiling rage. All of a sudden, the lights in the hall came on, the music lowering down slowly, showing out all of us from hiding, in the dark and most importantly, Tony kneeling right in front of Lisa, holding flowers, and a box of ring, open for her. Lisa gasped, dropping her jaws, tears rolling in her eyes, smile fighting its way through the infliction she had until then, as she looked at Tony.

"Lisa! Even though I scared you, will you marry me?" Tony asked, looking up at her. "And keep my head looking up always, just the way it is now?"

She let out a jolting smile of happiness and acceptance, and, "I will." She whispered, with a lowered voice almost choking out on her breath. Tony got up to his feet and lifted her up as she fled into his arms and the clapping of hands grew louder than the music. I could smell rejoice along with the aura of flowers and the room spray around us. The hall looked hazy and indistinct except Tony and Lisa. Ryna and Mitali dashed onto them to congratulate and celebrate.

As waking from a beautiful dream, I came back to the mysterious world after the celebrating dinner with my friends. I was lost again into the thoughts about Tim Koster. I felt desperate to finish the story. I called Daphne at ten in the night and she answered with a lazy voice. "Good morning!" she answered.

"It's ten in the night here." I said.

"I was going to call you. Mrs. Koster wouldn't say a

thing about Tim. She let me in, but she didn't want to talk about him." She went on.

"I'll be coming back to India next month." I said.

"Sure?"

"Yes. I have a few important exams in two weeks, and I'll come to India after that." I answered. I hung up after a fifteen-minute talk and crashed onto my bed. I could see my past, crystal clear, through the darkness in my bedroom. The sounds coming from the late night traffic that came through my window, seemed to faint as the deeper I thought. Tianna's voice in my head strangled me. All I could feel was the pricking in my heart. I fell asleep on my gloomy past and woke up the next day to follow the routine. Little did I know that love could change everything in a man's life. It could change a criminal to a humanitarian. It could change pleasantry to chaos. It could rise up hurdles on the path to happiness. It could show you an illusion where the sky and seas meet. Love could make people so naïve that knives are thought of as tools used just to chop vegetables. It could turn the cruel world to a fairyland. I then realized that it could never leave your eyes dry. Be it sadness, or happiness, they always tend to remain wet. Love is a win for the prevaricators, yet the other wins a life. All the hearts on fire, blind promises, and heart throbbing feelings would never go wasted. The burning up feeling deep inside the guts would only illuminate the gumption of the one who's caught in catastrophe. It is a halfway between heaven and hell.

I failed to avert my mind from Tianna and Tim. I did well in my exams though and dad booked tickets for my travel. "We can spend time with you later. Get this done now." He told me as he saw me off at the airport. "Finish what you started. This is not your job, not your career, not your life, but you chose a destiny to your passion, and Tim Koster is worth your precious time."

I gave him an approving smile and hugged him and mom from over the barricade. I walked away as mom shed tears and dad held her tight with his arm around her shoulder. I couldn't go ahead with the drafting of the story as I sat in the plane. I couldn't punch the keyboard of my laptop unless I knew the story. I waited patiently as I sat listening to music and watched movies on plane. I wished I could jump out of a window when the plane arrived at Mumbai. I didn't possess the patience to wait behind all the passengers who were boarding off the plane in my front.

#10

Anil and Daphne cameto receive me at the airport.I couldn't wait until the next day to talk to Tim Koster's parents.

"I spoke toMilie, a close friend of Saaya's." Daphne said. "She lives in Bangalore. After we talk to Kosters, we shall go on a road trip and see her this weekend."

"Excellent news my child." I remarked in a teasing manner, patting her head as we got into the car outside my parents' home.

"We tried after you left, Vian." Anil said as he drove and I sat behind them. "He's a ghost."

"I guess we need to get the story then." I gave out.

"Yes." Daphne agreed.

After a half an hour's drive, we found it to be thwarted, at the sight of the locked gates. "Damn it!" I let out a disappointing scowl. "I hope they're alright."

"They are scourged with whatever happened to Tim." Daphne saddened. "Poor Kosters."

I walked to the neighbor's gate and found the old man sitting in his garden. I pushed open the gate slowly and he noticed me enter. "Oh! You are Tim's friend, aren't you?" he asked, delighted to see me through his glasses, wrinkling his eyes with a smile. "How are you, son?"

"Why, I'm fine thank you. How about you? How are you doing?" I asked, walking towards him, trying to pretend that everything was fine.

"I'm doing just great. Thank you for asking." He replied warmly. "Are you here for the Kosters?" he questioned.

"Uh, umm-" I hesitatingly stuttered, with a blank mind. "Yes."

"They are away on a holiday to their hometown." He said. "They needed some time to calm things down."

"Oh, yeah I understand." I said. "Anyway, take care now. Have a pleasant evening."

"You too." He smiled at me as I turned to leave.

I decided to go to Bangalore to meet Saaya's friend and hoped that Kosters would be fine. I wished that I could talk to them and try consoling them. We sat in the car as we drove back to my parents' home, sowing the silence in our midst. The evening began to darken along with the gloom in our hearts. Time dragged by terribly slow and we counted every tick on the clock. We made reservations in a hotel in Bangalore and prepared for the trip. Milie, however booked a resort on Daphne's name so that she could spend the weekend with us and we had to cancel our reservation. The night was dark but was gloomier for me. That was the house where Tianna and I shared a lot of memories together whenever their family came over.

The next day, we drove along the NH4, taking turns with driving. We reached Bangalore by the dawn and checked in into the resort. We took a short nap before Milierung the bell to the block we were in. Daphne answered it before I walked out of the room which Anil and I had slept in. "Hey!" she hugged Daphnebefore she noticed me. "You changed a lot."

"Long time." Daphne exclaimed. "Milie, this is Vian. Vian! Milie." she introduced.

"Hi! Nice to meet you." I shook her hand.

"Daphne told me a lot about you. I'm glad to meet you."She said and turned to Daphne as she searched around the living room. "Where's Anil?"

"He's still asleep." I said, pointing my thumb to behind me where the door to the room was.

"He's not our senior anymore, is he?" Milie gave Daphne a hint with a wicked cunning smile and walked towards the bedroom. Daphne picked up a water bottle from the table across the room and walked in with Milie. I smiled at their plan of waking Anil up and followed them. By the time I could enter the room, I heard Anil shouting,

"What the hell?" and his face was wet with drops of water dripping down from his hairs. "Milie!" he exclaimed, with a mixed expression of surprise and irritation.

"How are you?"

"I'm wet." He scowled. He walked out along with them and settled on the couch with a lazy face as Daphne and Milie did some catching up of their own.

In the next hour that morning, we were sitting in Leela Palace enjoying a dulcet breakfast. Anil patiently waited for Daphne and me to begin the conversation and I wondered where to start. "So, what would you want to know about Saaya?" Milie popped up a question.

"Yes, I was about to ask. I will need your help regarding Saaya and Tim's story." I said, laying down my fork on the plate and looking up at her nervously.

"Certainly." She agreed.

"Well, can you tell us what you know of them?" I asked.

"Everybody knows about them." she plainly cut me off.

"I believe you are closer to her than anybody else. You must know her better." I pushed.

"Saaya was an unusual girl. She seemed to have dropped in from the 1980's. She definitely looked modern but she was old fashioned by heart." She started, eating her breakfast as she spoke. "We had been friends since school, so we got enrolled into the same college. We were summoned into an interaction with seniors on our way to class and Saaya was nervous. She incessantly wiped her palms though they weren't sweaty, and stared down at the ground. Koster noticed that she was uncomfortable and kept staring at her admirably as we were being asked numerous questions.

"Let 'em go." He said all of a sudden, when Saaya's

105

turn came up.

"What?" his classmates snapped, and gave him a surprised look.

"Let 'em go." He repeated, his eyes fixed at Saaya. We left them and their silenced desire to have fun and walked away to our classes. I turned back and saw Koster's continued gaze at Saaya. I was worried sick that he'd start hitting on her and play with her. At least that was how I heard about him. I was afraid that he would start stalking her forthwith. I was erred. He didn't. He did not bother to find out her name. Many a times did we pass by him, but all he did was glance at her with an adorable look and walk away. Saaya's impression on Koster wasn't positive a bit. That impression she had, induced in her a cautious and timid behavior. She ignored Koster in the eye and maintained a certain distance from him. But the things we ignore the most ends up imbed right beside us. Koster became good friends with her during the fresher party. Unremarkably, they exchanged numbers though Saaya hesitated to share her number with Koster in the start."

"Koster started calling her?" Daphne questioned, surprised and curious, interrupting Milie. Anil shot her an annoyed look and, "Ok. Sorry. Go on."

"Koster didn't call her. He never even sent her a text either. Saaya only had an extra contact number in her mobile and so did Koster." Milie continued. "A third year guy came in Saaya's way to her lab one day and attempted to introduce himself. He was not harsh but his over pretense of sweetness was disquieting to Saaya. She sent a text to Koster without him noticing as he tried to get her to talk. She later told me that she sent him, 'Second floor, physics lab, help.'

"I'm getting late for the lab." Saaya gave him an excuse. He stepped aside to give her way but walked with her.

"I'll walk you to the lab if you don't mind." He insisted but Koster met them on the way.

"Saaya? You got a minute?" Koster called. *"Something important."*

"Sure." Saaya agreed readily.

"Koster. Would you please leave?" the senior tried to warn him.

"I'm here to talk to her. Don't make me deal with you." Koster warned upfront. Saaya paced up her steps alongside Koster leaving behind the senior and walked to the lab.

"That's your lab. Ciao!" Koster saw her off with a smile and I was stunned to see her smiling back at him. As soon as she walked in, I asked her if something was going on and she told me what had happened.

"He's not as bad as we thought, you know?" Saaya said with her sweetest voice as she pulled out her record books. I doubted that Koster was up to something. I was suspicious and afraid that he was going to hurt her. I was extremely right. He got her to fall for him. It took him long but he did it, and broke her heart." She finished, foreshortening the story.

"What?" Daphne snarled. "She was the one who dumped him."

"No. Koster did it. Her acceptance to marry her cousin is her behavior in one of the bad tempers. Her failure to get married to Koster ensued with her adapting to her family's decision.Koster regretted his mistake when he heard of her engagement and crumpled. There was nothing he could do to get her back. He then met with an accident and died. Saaya has got no flaw in this." Milie finished.

I fell back and leaned on my chair puzzled and shocked. "How did he woe Saaya?" I questioned.

"He flirted, showed her a false world, dipped her in imaginary sweetness and a lot other things. Just the way he trapped Gargi and Asna, as a matter of fact." She scoffed.

"No. Saaya was the one who was behind Koster." Daphne made an attempt to defend Koster.

"I had been Saaya's shadow." Milie argued. I could do nothing but sit stuck to my chair frozen with suspended thoughts. I wasn't surprised anymore to hear about ten versions of a story.

"Weren't they happy together?" I asked Milie while we went shopping later that noon. Anil and Daphne were busy searching for what they wanted to shop.

"Yes." she answered. "But it was only one of them; Saaya. Koster only pretended to be happy with her."

"He wouldn't do that." I contended, looking down at the ground floor from the top, with my hands on the handrail.

"What do you know about the devil in Koster?" she asked in a flouting manner. "Saaya was just another number for him. She was a mere memento of victory." She continued to loathe Koster.

"Is there a possibility of meeting Saaya?" I asked.

"She wouldn't even meet me." Milie cut me off.

We didn't revel in the trip to meet Milie except she was a nice person. It exposed a decayed part of the story, nevertheless my interest in the truthful story remained unfeigned. We had been opined that Tim was abandoned by Saaya. Saaya was not to be blamed completely, if Milie's story was true. I just sat dead in the car on our way back to Mumbai that night. Every person had a different point of view on Tim Koster. It started getting hard for me to figure out which of those was the actual truth. The trip wasn't tiresome. Nevertheless, all I did was think about whatever we have found so far and I tried to piece it all together to analyze the truth. I fell asleep as Anil drove without even blinking his eyes. Daphne leaned back in the rear seat and dozed off too.

#11

After a few more bootless trails to meet Saaya or unveiling Tim Koster's story, I returned back to New York for Tony and Lisa's wedding and got busy with my parents. My drafting Tim Koster conked gradually, as the time passed and I found myself busy with many other activities. His story remained just another tragically mysterious one. Tony's time with us thinned down after his marriage with Lisa. Ryna and Mitali would come around once in a while and spend time with my parents and me.

I was mostly repressed and Uncle Silburn called me often just to hear an excuse that I needed more time. He insisted that I intermit on Koster's story and work on the other two prior fictions I had written. Well I have tried but Tim Koster's sorrow imprints were conflating with a fantasy theme of my fiction. A month passed by and my parents returned back to India to take care of the businesses. Time began to eat up the light in my life and grew harder on me. Every time I decided upon working on dropping a line in the story, I only ended up looking at the document on my computer attentively.

Our Master's program came to an end and Ryna and

Mitali's family were working on their wedding date. Fixing a date for a wedding in India is the hardest part. I never got a chance to go to bottom of it though. I contemplated getting out of Koster's story for a while. Dad offered to help Mitali's parents for the wedding arrangements along with Ryna's family. Since I failed to ponder with my book, I booked my travel tickets to India along with Ryna and Mitali for their wedding. We would be leaving to India in a week and I received a call while I was at dinner with friends one night.

"You better catch your next flight to India and get your ass down here." Daphne shouted over the phone as I answered it. I didn't ask any question, but patiently waited for the dinner to end, grabbed my jacket and hurried to my car. I jumped in and searched for availability of tickets over the internet as I drove. Daphne's voice sounded shaken up. I had a feeling deep in my guts that it's something important and suspected if it was about Tim Koster. Until that moment, I never realized that I had already taken this very seriously. I was caught in the grip of that moment and felt that I had to get it done no matter what. Unfortunately, I managed to get a flight for the next night.I looked fagged after an hour of packing my bags for the trip. I wasn't certain how many days I was going to be away. Anyhow, Ryna and Mitali'swedding was going to be held in Mumbai. So I sent them a text that I left early.

I was waiting for the flight the next evening when Anil called me. He spoke with great fervor over the phone. His voice felt heavy with triumphant news. I was peculiarly tensed about what might have popped up.

"Dude. When are you going to reach?" he asked.

"I'll be there by tomorrow."

111

The way I ran to board the plane at half past eight seemed like I was a first timer. I sat in a British Airways plane tired and weary, but couldn't sleep with many questions running in my head.After a delicious breakfast and tautness at the London Heathrow Airport the next morning, I boarded a connecting flight to Mumbai. With a great effort, I toppled into deep sleep and reached Mumbai at around midnight. Anil and Daphne came along with my parents to receive me.

"They got something for you." Dad said, giving me a hug after mom loosened her arms around me.

"What is it?" I asked Anil, turning to Daphne and him. Daphne moved around excited and commoved, with a glint in her eyes.

"Saaya got married to her cousin three days ago." Anil spoke out quickly.

"So?"

"Something happened at the wedding."

"Or rather someone." Daphne interrupted, unable to hide the blush in her face.

"Koster? TIM KOSTER?" I shouted, with a high pitched voice, drawing everybody's attention in the airport. I turned to the disturbed passengers, gestured them an apology and turned back to Anil and Daphne. "Tim Koster?" I repeated in a lowered tone.

"Yes, but he disappeared again." Anil said changing his face to disappointment.

"But he came didn't he?" I questioned.

"I suppose, yes."

"He's alright?"

"I don't know. We haven't seen him. We heard that he slightly limped due to an injury in the leg which impeded his movement, but he looked totally fine."

"And we still can't meet him, even after we know that he exists?"

"No."

"Saaya croaked and went into a shock on seeing him. Her fiancé already knew the story so he was barely petrified." Daphne gave in. "Neetu and I shook her back to normal and she agreed to talk to you about him next month."

"Why the wait?"

"Well, she'd be going on a honeymoon." Daphne said with a ridiculous sound and rolled her eyes.

"That's-" I paused, going dummy all of a sudden. "Ok. I want to meet someone who can talk to me about Tim Koster." I instructed.

"Hell, everybody will talk, now that Tim returned." Anil assured. I turned to dad enraptured. He looked into my eyes with a lofty stare and,

"I guess you are going to have to stay for a long time, now." He snatched the baggage trolley from me and rolled it with him in his front as we walked out together.

I was filled with a sudden urge to set out on an interminable journey to drag out Koster's story. It wasn't my passion that compelled me. It wasn't my selfish attempt to publish my book. It wasn't my curiosity. I felt that I was indebted to Koster. I longed for his story to break out of inviolable situation. I felt that knowing him would help me find myself. 'I might as well expect to talk to Saaya's parents in the morning.' I thought. I was relieved that I wouldn't need to get accustomed to people not wanting to talk about Tim. I yearned to get to the snob in Tim Koster. I decided to adjudicate Tim's blotting out by feeding on truth and conclusive evidence. The withered love between Saaya and Tim needed to be worth their lives apart. The bliss in their relation may not have disgorged, but it wouldn't have had to go wasted. The vibes in their midst should be felt by everyone. I could already smell the air and tell that I was back at home. It was filled with compassionate love, sentimental and ample.

After so long, I was able to sleep pleasantly although it was for a short time after reaching home at 2 A.M. in the morning. I woke up to Daphne's racket outside from the living room. I lied down still, my eyes wide open and rolled off the bed to my feet.I walked in a lively manner, with enthusiasm kicking out smiles over my face.

We had a quick breakfast and set off to Saaya's house. Anil steered while I sat beside him and Daphne took the rear seat. We didn't talk to each other all the way. I was preparing myself on how to constitute the story based on the facts I was going to hear. I was preparing myself on the appropriate questions to be asked.

"You didn't hang around after the wedding?" Mrs. Viroodh asked Daphne as we got out of the car in front of the main door."Come on in. I'll arrange breakfast for you guys."

"We already had." Daphne politely denied. Mrs.

Viroodh escorted us to inside the spacious living room where Mr. Viroodh was seated. He stood up to greet us, and gave his hand to me for a shake.

"Vian!" he called, shaking my hand gently. "Daphne told me about you. How was the journey?"

"It was pleasant." I answered. The house was swarming with voices and calls of people around, unpacking, removing the decorations, et cetera. I could sense ruefulness in Mr. Viroodh's eyes. Perhaps it was due to the sudden appearance of Tim Koster at the wedding. "Is everything alright?" I asked him, maintaining my eye contact with his.

"What-? Uh- Oh! It's nothing." He stammered, pulling himself back to senses. "I saw Koster at my daughter's wedding."

"So I heard." I said. "About his attending the wedding."

"It was supposed to be his wedding." Mr. Viroodh grumbled calmly, his eyes, staring blank at the floor.

"Do you mind telling us what happened?" I requested.

"My daughter fell in love with Koster. She told me the moment she knew she was in love with him. But my wife gave her word to her brother that she'd marry his son to Saaya. There were conflictions between my wife and me, but she wouldn't hitch Saaya's happiness either. We never knew how it all happened; how they fell in love, and why they broke up. I certainly observed that they had issues before they broke up. My daughter was broken. She made up her mind to marry her mother's choice. We also had discussions

115

with the Kosters about the wedding and they were overwhelmed. They waited for Saaya to join their family. Nonetheless, after the breakup, Saaya wouldn't even want to hear the sound of Tim. The negative reputation he had prior to his relation with Saaya, made me do what my daughter wanted and got her engaged. Tim showed up at the engagement. He was totally embarrassed but that didn't bother him at all. All he could think of, was Saaya's being engaged. The look in his eyes told me that he didn't want to lose Saaya. I stepped forward to bring him in but,

"*Please.*" He muttered to me and turned to Saaya. Breathing heavily and looking straight at my daughter. "*I hope I will be there, to tell you, 'I told you so.'*" He out-cried to her. He glared at her for a few seconds and left, with a rage.

I questioned Saaya to tell me what exactly happened but she wouldn't. She was as furious as Tim was.I went to meet the Kosters the very evening but they wouldn't say anything either. I thought they were mad at us.I later heard that he met with an accident on his way back from the engagement. When I questioned Saaya and told her about the accident, "*I don't care even if he dies.*" She screamed and went into her room. Mr. Koster wouldn't pick my call and I never got to know what really happened between them." He finished.

"How did Tim react at the wedding?" I questioned.

"I waited for something magical to happen. I waited for either of them to make a move. He quietly sat in a chair, watched the ceremony and left."

"What's your opinion about him?"

"Well he's from overseas, wonted to the western

culture, but he was a nice guy. I inquired about him before I talked to Kosters and people told me he was pretty serious about marrying Saaya. I met him a couple of times; handsome, talkative, frank, polite, well-mannered, and a gentleman." Mr. Viroodh finished.

"Do you think he dumped Saaya and that's what made her aggressive?"

"I'm unsure about it I must say. On the other hand, I'm glad that Tim came back."

Mrs. Viroodh served us with juice, which we accepted readily.

"If you happen to meet the Kosters," Mr. Viroodh said, "tell them we're sorry, although it doesn't cover anything. That's the least I can do."

I nodded agreeing to him as I sipped on the juice. "Certainly."

#12

It took us one hour to reach Kosters' from Viroodhs'. My expectation of the story obliterated. It remained shrouded. Kosters' gates didn't have the locks on them, and the watchman hurriedly opened the gate as our car drove to it. Surprised with the unexpected warm welcome, we drove in through the gate along the path between the gardened front yards, and pulled bybeside Kosters' car. I expected to meet Tim in there although Daphne told me he disappeared again. A miniscule hope remained in me that Tim would still be there, spending time with his parents.A maid in her late thirties answered the door as we rang the doorbell and motioned us in. Mr. Koster came walking to the living room in his trousers and tees and requested us to be seated.

"Please be seated."

"I'm Vian." I introduced myself. Mitali's friend. We came by couple of months ago, but-" I paused. I could still remember his face from my last visit where he spoke to us through the window of his car. He looked politer in person. His glasses made him look like a professor in some university.

"Oh! Yes. Mitali. I remember seeing you with them." he said. "Mr. Rao sent us an invitation for her wedding next month. How's she?"

"She's doing great."

"I apologize Daph!" he turned to Daphne as we sat down. "We were a little off course after Tim got hurt."

"Is he still here?" I asked, eagerly, eyeing around the house, and taking a glance at the shoe shelf, trying to spot one of his pairs though I was incognizant of his taste.

"He went back to where he came from." Mr. Rao said quickly, or probably lied.

"Can you tell us where he is? It's important that we talk to him."

"I'm afraid I can't. He just needs some time. I don't want him bothered."

Mr. Rao was either telling us the truth that Tim made sure they wouldn't hold any information about him, or it was all a trivial lie. Since it wouldn't be polite to push, I dropped the idea of asking them for Tim's contact.

"We have met Mr. Viroodh and he sends his apologies." I conveyed.

"Yes. It was Tim's fault too. It's unfair to blame them completely." Mr. Koster said.

"Can you tell us what exactly happened?" I asked, as Daphne denied taking some food items the maid brought. We were already tummy full by then.

"Tim didn't tell us anything about the fight but he sure enough lost his tongue and said things which he wasn't supposed to. They fought with each other and wanted to break up but Tim only acted out of his extreme rage and choler. I heard him plead her and cry over the phone at nights, but he never disclosed anything to us. He wanted to ensure they'd fix it back. Saaya changed his life. She made him sweeter and softer. Tim followed and got habituated to our traditions and customs. He started to believe in God. He avoided getting into troubles and we felt so secured about him. He would kiss his mom every evening after he returned from college. He learned to cook and helped his mother in the kitchen, so that he would cook for Saaya. From a spoilt brat, he turned into a complete upright and respectable man with ethical values.He started to believe that blessings favored him more, rather than luck and money. Saaya was his remediation. She made him believe that true love is the remedy to every suffering. Yet, they failed to cope with a mere start of their wrangles. They didn't have the strength to fight to be together." Mr. Koster went on.

"Do you know how, they started to be fond of each other?"

"Tim never told us anything. He only depicted that he was happy with her and that was all we wanted; his happiness."

"What happened afterwards?"

"They fought, broke up, and for some reason, Saaya got engaged to her cousin. I was vexed at Mr. Viroodh that he let such a thing happen and my son was torn apart."

Kosters weren't able to provide us with much information. We reached home in the evening before the darkness fell, and mom was totally engaged in preparing delicious dinner. I was still stuck in a circular maze. The inner circle dampened me with Tianna's memories and outer with my not being so successful with Tim's trail.

"Vincent!" Anil shouted, while we were having dinner, clapping his hands for once but loudly, which scared us all. "Oh ho. Vincent!" he repeated.

"Vincent who?" I asked him curiously.

"Tim's best friend from outside the college."

"Do you know him?"

"No. He once interfered in our seniors' fight with Tim in our college."

"You are Tim's senior, aren't you? And he fought with your seniors?"

"He's a hard one." Anil remarked.

"How do we find him?" I asked.

Anil shrugged his shoulders and nodded his head sideways. I looked away from him and continued eating. "Wait!" I snapped looking back at him with incertitude, shrinking my eyes. "I bet he's on Facebook."

"Yes." Anil exclaimed. "Let's give it a try."

The three of us were stuck to my desk and Anil logged into his Facebook account. He checked the notifications and found a friend request. "Who'd send request to me?" he gagged himself as he clicked on it and found Milie's pending request.

"Anil? Vincent!" Daphne reminded him.

"One moment please. I'm actually surprised that people send requests to me."

He stood there bent forward, surprised and excited, his emotions stirred, as he accepted Milie's friend request.

"She sent you a friend request. Not marriage proposal." Daphne made a wooing sound to tease him and he quickly closed it to search for Vincent. '*Vincent*' he typed in the search column and a Vincent Denier's profile was suggested, displaying Tim Koster in mutual friends.He sent a request and a message briefing him about the situation. We then schmoosed for a while to kill time and Daphne fell asleep on my bed. Anil and I took the other room for the night. He had fallen asleep right after he closed his eyes, but I stayed up staring into the dark. I wanted to find something; something which would absorb all the greed in me for everything else. I wanted to find something which would make me forget Tianna. I wanted to get busy and involved into an activity or ferment which would roll me away from her. I never thought getting over a breakup was so hard and unwieldy. All the same, I hoped that Tianna would lead a very happy life and I was sure that she had moved on.

I fought with my memories and thoughts to fall asleep. The weight of the sorrows increasing, I sunk into worst nightmares which shook me awake at 4 in the morning. Lighting a cigar, I walked into the balcony and listened to songs in my iPod. I suddenly noticed from the balcony after about an hour, Daphne sneaking out through the main door downstairs. She walked into the garden in the front yard and seated herself on the swing. I pulled out my mobile and dialed her number, observing her through the fading darkness of the morning.

"What are you doing out there?" I asked.

"Couldn't sleep." She answered, looking around to spot me.

"Hang on. I'm coming."

I tip toed out of the room careful not to disturb Anil, climbed down the stairs and then out the front door. The grass in the garden was damp and soft. The fog wet my flip flops as I tramped on it to reach Daphne. Daphne's face looked shriveled in the dim light falling from a street light outside the compound wall.

"What's wrong?" I asked as she moved aside on the swing to give room for me to sit.

"Nightmares." She said. "Were you in the balcony?"

"Yes. I saw you coming out and called you."

"Oh!"

"Do you think we'd be able to find Vincent?" I asked.

"I hope we do. If he is Koster's best friend, he might be able to tell us a lot about Saaya and him." I nodded to her and looked into her eyes with admiration. Her voice sounded comforting. She continued to talk lazily, but occupied with details and moving. "Is it Tianna?" she asked all of a sudden.

"What?"

"Is it because of her that you can't sleep?"

"Oh, huh, umm, it's Tim actually. But yes, Tianna too, of course." I stuttered.

123

"Don't worry. Just try to deviate your mind." She spoke with her softest voice, piercing the words so thin through her lips.

"Let alone Tianna in my past, I repent for her memories I drown in."

"Did you smoke?" she asked, smiling at me. I looked away at the sunrays coming out of the distant ground with the sun still hidden. "And Mitali told me that your alcohol consumption has gone high lately."

"Yes." I answered abashed. "These certain unsuitable addictions make every pain sweet to me."

"You will find something soon which will make you stop all that." She stated, gripping my hand tighter. "Come on. I shall make coffee to erase that cigarette stench." We walked into the house as the sun came up from between the trees into the dull sky.

In one of the days next week, we were driving to a car racing club at Bandra in Mumbai to meet Vincent. He replied to Anil's message on Facebook early that morning and agreed to meet personally. I sat behind Anil and Daphne in the rear seat lost in my thoughts. I wanted those hard times of sleeping wide awake to end. I wanted to confront Tianna's damage and get a life. I jolted awake as Anil applied hard brakes at the parking. Anil dialed to Vincent as he stepped out and a guy in early twenties, walked over to him. He looked too simple, rough hair dyed in brown, a plain t-shirt and jeans. He looked tanned. He didn't look like a guy who gave a damn about maintaining his looks.

"Anil?" he called. "Vince!" he offered his hand for a shake.

"Hey, hi. This is Vian and that's Daphne." He introduced us.

"Oh! Vian. Mr. Koster told me about you the other day."

"I'm glad to meet you." I said shaking his hand.

"Likewise." He smiled, "can we, uh talk over some breakfast? I'm hungry as a cat."

We were seated comfortably in Café Basilico for breakfast and Vincent ordered for his breakfast. "Do you know where Koster is?" Anil asked without wasting any time.

"He's in New Delhi." Vince answered quickly.

"Delhi?" We snapped together, Anil and I.

"Yup."

"What's he doing there?" I gave in.

"He didn't tell me. I only hope that he's fine."

"Can you tell us anything about Saaya and him?"

"He never spoke of Saaya. He kept it all to himself. Not a word about her but he did mention her name." he started. "I met Koster in the race club. He was excessively occupied with racing and stuff.His eyes showed what he had in his mind. He never faked anything. I started to like him though he's forthright. We're more like brothers. We raced together once in a while.Most people could only give you a fabricated story. Saaya should be back in a week. She is the only one apart from Tim, who can give you the true story, or probably most of it."

"I'm asking you out of curiosity." I started but paused for a while, and Vince was keenly waiting for me to continue. "How did Tim fall in love with Saaya?"

"He never knew." Vince snapped. "Not even when Saaya cried out for him to be with her."

"I don't understand."

"It was something beyond love. He failed to realize that." Vince went on. "He was in love. But he never had a picture of her with him, never tried to meet her, hell; he didn't even call her on the phone in the beginning."

"How did they get together?" I asked, listening to him fervently.

"He never spoke of it. He maintained a very private relation with her. She would ask him to meet and he would race away. He would lose track of time talking to her over the phone. Tim Koster, was Saaya Viroodh's fairy tale; and she was his angel. I liked her too. She was so sweet. They looked cute together. All I did was back him up a couple of times when he had an issue with his seniors. He was a hard one. He was never afraid to take beating and we can rarely find people like that. He knows how to hit 'em back, one by one."

"Are you sure he's in Delhi?" Anil asked. "We thought no one ever knew. Mr. Koster didn't know either."

"Yes, that's because Kosters are too soft on Saaya and he didn't want them to slip their tongues to her, of his whereabouts. And he's not a frigging criminal that no one could find him. He's just a man who's hurt and broke." Vince teased.

"Where does he live in Delhi?" I questioned.

"He didn't tell me that." He answered sharply. "The only time I saw fear in him was when he fell in love with Saaya. He was afraid and frightened of how to react to her. He was afraid of losing her. Apart from that, he left everything very obscure." We sat there for a while longer chatting and got up to leave. We walked out of there talking to each other as Vince hurried away.

We saw him race off in his Porsche 911 GT2 with the engine purring. We then got into our car and drove back to my home. I couldn't wait for Saaya to return and narrate me the story accurately. I logged onto Facebook that evening and came across Tianna's photo updates on my home page. Turning indocile, I clicked on the pictures and viewed them. They were her pictures with her husband, happy and sound, cheerful and joyous. Daphne suddenly walked into the room and,

"Saaya is coming home this Sunday." She shouted from the door. Then, "Vian?" she called silently, walking in to me. "Shut it down and come out for some air. Mom and dad want us home for dinner."

"Sure." I replied. "I'll be out in a jiffy."

"Now, you don't have to do that." She pulled me by my hand, closing down the LCD lid of my laptop with a gentle thud. We spent some time out in the garden with mom and dad and got back in when the sunlight perished. Dinner with Daphne's parents was idyllic. Anil began to get busy chatting with Milie all the time and his face was mostly covered in unnoticeable smiles and grins which turned the color of his cheeks. Well, Daphne teased but all he could do was blush and look back into his mobile as if he were about to dig something out of it.

#13

My stomach stirred with a lot of feelings the following Sunday; anxiety, curiosity, veneration towards love between Saaya and Tim and commiseration for them. I sat in the car tapping my feet nervously as we approached Saaya Viroodh's house. I could hear my heartbeat as loud as a thunder. I was afraid that I might drown in my own sweat and choke on my fears. I was horrified about how the story would go. Anil yanked open the door pulling me back from imaginary world and let me out. Mr. Viroodh was waiting to receive us at the front door. "Saaya?" he called out with his quavered tone.

She stuck her head out from the kitchen door across the hallway and then walked out. She was indeed beautiful. No wonder she was Tim's angel. I knew then, why Tim was marveled at the sight of her from the very beginning. I acknowledged how one could remain awestruck at her charming face. "How are you?" she opened her mouth ajar as she hugged Daphne. "Hey Anil!" she then looked at me indifferently and,

"Hi I'm Vian Bansi!" I introduced myself shaking her hand.

"Oh, yes." She greeted with a simplest yet sweet smile. "I was informed that you would be expected." I was dumbfounded of how Saaya could have so rigid a heart to depart from Tim. Perhaps I had to wait to hear the story for the answer. She made us a toothsome cold coffee topped with ice cream and led us onto the terrace. The climate being cloudy and pleasant, the smell of the air was teeming. "I probably have an hour or two before my husband returns, and I don't want to make him uncomfortable with Tim's talk."

I saw Daphne go slightly red in face which she covered up insignificantly. She gave me an apathetic look and turned back to Saaya. "Do you know where Koster is?" she shot a question straight into her face.

"New Delhi." Saaya sighed, looking at the floor.

"How do you know?" Daphne asked bewildered.

"Well at some point, he needed to reserve tickets to go somewhere. I have contacts that can get me certain information like that based on a name and age." She boldly answered.

"I want you to understand that this is entirely based on Tim and you are a huge part of his life who can tell us a lot more than anybody else at all." I lied.

"Yes, I understand." She agreed, timidly.

"Can you tell me how, you guys got along?" I asked.

"Milie was the only friend I had back then and I was

very fearful of seniors. We were called the moment we walked into the campus and I almost felt like I was going to have a nervous breakdown." She started. "Tim's friends kept questioning Milie and my fear range boosted up after every single question that I was going to be next. I had an impulse to run away from there and plead dad to enroll me into a women's college. I stood there rubbing the moist that formed on my hands and looking at my own feet, trying telepathy on them to make a move and run. *"Let 'em go."* I heard a steady voice from one of them. Tim's friend didn't want to give up so soon but Tim insisted that they let us go. I hurried away with Milie following me.

"I can sense that there's something wrong with that guy." She said, looking back as we walked away to our class. *"You better be careful girl."* I wasn't disobliged by her warning but was relieved that they let us go for the moment. The gossip about Tim reached far enough and twisted into my ears later and Milie warned me to be more careful about him. She told me of the way he stared at me during my first day in college. Although I always had my head bent down, I could locate him by his voice. I could tell how far away he would be from me, from the loudness of his voice without taking a look around. My evasive behavior around him only absorbed the fears within me. He neither stalked me nor disturbed me in any way. I have only been warned of something which never existed.I saw him with Nevan a couple of times. Tim would have Nevan's back every time someone tried to pull in on him. He wasn't arrogant as people called him. He was only used to a luxurious life and fun. His interaction with us during fresher's party was very polite and friendly accord. He treated us with regard.

I noticed Tim walking towardsme and looked down choppily. *"Something wrong with the ground?"* He spoke, taking his position beside me as we stood watching some cultural events on stage. *"You can look up and have fun. Do not worry about anything."*

"I tend to remain scared in the beginning." I said in a silent tone, shyly.

"Beginning is long gone now. No harm's going to come to you around here. Everyone is very friendly; you can be free, turn to any of us for help. We don't treat you people as lunch and we're definitely not hungry." He tried to boost up my confidence.

"Can I have your number?" I asked, *"Just in case."*

"Yeah sure." He agreed and we exchanged numbers. My fears weren't dead yet. I was worried and afraid. I was nervous to talk to him. Somehow, I took that friendly appeal as a sign of Tim's hitting on me. I took his number so that I would know that it was him if he called and I wouldn't answer."

Daphne started making irritated faces unnoticed by Saaya while she was busy looking down as she narrated. Anil pulled out a box of cigarettes and looked at Saaya if it was ok to smoke. Saaya nodded him to go ahead and Anil's face lit as if he had passed through an exam. He pulled out a cigarette from the box, lit it with his lighter and stuffed the box and lighter back into his pocket.

"Every time my mobile rang or received a message, I was frightened that it was Tim and that he'd start bothering me. But he never did call or text me. I almost felt like I was waiting for him to call me." Saaya went on. "I started observing him at college. He would be busy and he never gazed or stared at me. Mostly it was just a short glance sometimes. I wondered if I was disappointed. I was

132

sometimes spurred to call him or send him a message and talk. It was very hard, not to. I would calm myself down and go on with my work. I was one day late to college and walking to the lab alone. A third year guy came into my path and tried pretending to be sweet. I felt fazed and deviled. He wasn't rude but his pretense was unbearable. I needed help and Tim was the one who crossed my mind right away. I sent him a text asking him to help me out by the lab and he got me out of there. I called him again in the evening to thank him and spoke for a few minutes. His talk was clear and straight. It didn't contain any hidden intentions.

"Thank you for helping me out today." I said.

"Don't mention it."

"So what's up? What are you doing?" I asked.

"I just got home. What about you?"

"Me too. Just wanted to say thank you."

"That's alright. Take care." He said and hung up. I wondered if he didn't want to talk to me but then I realized that he just reached home and he must have been tired just as I was with all the classes and lab work.He didn't turn up in college for a few days after that. I later heard that he got into some kind of row with our seniors and they beat him up. There was this guy Vincent-"

"We met him." Anil interrupted.

"Oh!" she sighed nodding her head slowly and got back to the story. "Vince was his friend from a race club. Tim rammed into a guy's car and beat him up outside college. No, this is not the incident with the one from your batch." She told Anil when he gave her a sudden familiar look as if he knew what she was talking about. "He was set up by your seniors. It started with the guy who bothered me at the lab. Vince got back at one of them but more waited the next day. I wasn't aware of all that. I was from a different block in college. Vince joined Tim along with his friends and Tim's way of fighting back made them cede the fight and they knew better to stay out of his way. They knew that Tim's friends could do a lot of damage. I called Tim the moment I heard of it and he spoke like it was no big deal and those types of issues were common in college. *"Can I come to see you?"* I asked.

"Sure. I will ask Asna to bring you along from college." He said.

I knew that he was with Asna and they were not going to end up together forever. I was glad that he was a good friend to me and hoped he would remain same. At 5 in the evening, I was headed to Tim's house along with Asna. She wasn't such a girl as the rumors had it. She was very friendly and frank. She was definitely not in love with Tim.

"Did you know that he got involved into this for you?" she asked me as she drove, smiling at me. I nodded yes to her and looked at the road in front. *"Don't worry. He's fine. He's just had a few bruises."* I only remained calm without saying a word. *"He doesn't talk to anyone these days. I wonder what's wrong with him."*

Kosters made me feel at home with their hospitality. Tim was fine but he had bruises on his hands and his knuckles were slightly injured and red in color.

"She's worth the fight." Mr. Koster joked as he saw Tim struggle to sit on the couch with his strained knee.

134

"Dad?"

Tim showed me around the house and then took me onto the terrace with Asna helping him crawl up the stairs by his arm. *"I'll get us some coffee."* Asna said, turning back and disappeared down the staircase.

"Do your parents know about you guys?" I asked nervously and puzzled.

Tim shot a cold smile as if I were innocent and nodded. *"We're just cool with each other. We're not into a relation."*

I looked down at the ground from over the terrace as I searched for words to talk to him.*"I love you."* He said all of a sudden, almost freezing me to death.

"What?"

"Didn't you hear me? Or do you want me to repeat it?" he asked, looking into my eyes. I looked back straight into his eyes fearlessly and read that he wasn't lying. I shifted my stare from his one eye to the other while he pierced his gaze deep into both of mine. He was irresistible. The charm in his face was overpoweringly attractive. I looked away with a sudden jerk when I noticed Asna appear at the terrace while Tim continued to stare at me. She was holding for us a tray in which the coffee cups were and Tim and I took one each. She took her cup and placed the tray on the tea table beside us. I tried to hide my face filled with guilt and fear. Tim continued to smile unobtrusively and my heart thumped with fright, worried how Asna would react if she had found out what happened.

"What's wrong?" Asna asked, looking at us both. I turned to look at her and Tim was frozen smiling at me. It

was kind of irritating though, but I was gasping with a dead brain. I knew Tim wouldn't lie, but the truth would scathe her.

"I just-"

"He was trying to tease me." I crossed him off from telling her the truth. *"Can you drop me home? I'm getting late. It just struck my mind that I have to go shopping with mom."* I lied with a flimsy stammer.

"Yeah, sure." She agreed indifferently looking at Tim. We rushed down the stairs with them close behind me, so that Tim wouldn't spill the beans out to Asna. I felt like my heart would drop down, until Asna got into the car beside me and we drove out of their gate. *"Why are you so afraid?"* she asked as we drove. *"He is of no harm. Calm down now."*

"Yeah, I tend to become nervous sometimes, that's all." I tried to conceal my fears.

"I think he's into you." Asna snapped all of a sudden smiling at me.

"What!!!"

"Relax! I'm not sure. I just think he is. I know him well enough but I'm not really sure."

"I thought you guys were-" I started to doubt.

"Together?" she asked and chuckled at me. *"We had that talk but we found out we're really better off as friends."*

"I don't understand."

"Tim, he's complicated. I thought he was into me and I kinda was slightly attracted to him in the start to be honest with

136

you. But then as I got closer to him, he likes me as a person and loves my company. I share everything with him. I'm just comfortable with him. Simple as that."

"But everyone thinks that-" I tried to tell her.

"I know. We know. Some dumb rumors aren't going to create a relation that doesn't exist between us, and neither can they break us."

I looked to my front and my eyes became tenderly delicate to see anything. I was hit with a storm of surprise about how Asna could be so calm. Or maybe they were really just good friends. I realized that what we see and what we hear are two entirely different things. I couldn't wait to reach home and fall asleep so that after I woke up, I could take it all to be a bad dream and get over it.Tim didn't show any signs of bothering me the following day. It was all back to normal again and I was perplexed, if it was really a bad dream. He was with Mitali when I called him in the evening and,

"Hi." I spoke with an eerie feeling. *"Can you come over to have some coffee?"*

"Sure, why not." He agreed and, *"Mitali! I gotta go. See you guys tomorrow."* I heard his voice sounding distant from the phone. I met him at the parking and we drove to the café. I ordered a White Chocolate Mocca and Tim a cappuccino.

"Can I ask you something?" I asked, hesitatingly, with a foreboding that it was actually a bad idea.

"Go ahead."

"Did I come to your home yesterday evening?"

"Have you been drinking?"

"No, I just am surprised if that really happened."

"For your kind information, it did; and I hope you're not on drugs." He teased, but I was unable to laugh. I was scared and affright. *"Now stop worrying and drink up your coffee. I got some work with dad and I'll drop you home safe before I hurry."*

"I was afraid you would tell Asna about it. Poor girl would have got hurt if you did."

"She won't be. She's more like my twin soul and not just a friend. Everyone's got this wrong and I hope you won't be one of them."

He motioned me up from the table when he got a call from his dad and dropped me home safe and secure. *"Take care now. Ciao."* He said, as I got down the car. I nodded to him with a steadfast face through the window and saw his car drive away. I walked into the house after his car disappeared out of my sight. I sent him a text after dinner that night thanking him for the coffee. He replied to me right away as if he was readily waiting for my message. It went on for a while and the clock ticked days like seconds. Months and years passed and I would talk to him every single day and he never showed any imperativeness. He never flirted with me nor did his way of talk showed toying. I began to turn deaf with my ears to his heart and adapt my trust in him. It was like an omen that was bound to happen sooner or later. Mitali too started talking to me. We would hang out for coffee, movies and shopping, but he was perpetually formal with me though he treated me with utmost love and care. I would hold him by his arm and walk while he only smiled at me. He would make me laugh and I'd plead him to talk to me for a while longer every day over the phone. He would fall asleep with me talking to him over the phone. I would call him again and try wake him up, but he would be sound asleep by then. I would make a crying face the next morning and he would apologize to me sweetly. I had always been impatient until I shared every incident or gossip with him. I had started to dissolve into him. I woke up to the sound of his silent love. I'm ignorant if there were heaven and hell but I believed in Tim Koster. Smoothening music was no longer necessary. His voice, lit me up too bright."

#14

Saaya's face turned pallid all of sudden and her mind seemed to rove into the past which she had almost forgot. We only stayed still, observing her and waited for her to continue. Anil threw away his cigarette and delivered his seriousness into the cold evening. Daphne turned to me wondering if Saaya was fine. Saaya respired, as if sucking in life that existed in the air around her.

"Tim realized that I had fallen for him. Mitali warned me to stay away from him though she was his best friend. *"You're only going to end up getting hurt."* She said.

"What do you mean?" I asked.

"Koster is a very good guy. But he doesn't know how to handle a relation. That's one reason why he tries blending in with people; why he's always choosy about his friends."

We were sitting in the beach where she asked me to meet. Her warning words made a clonking sound in my heart. *"I still don't understand what you're trying to say."*

"He's afraid of relationships because of which he walks away. Did you ever wonder why he had to come back to India? He

had to go through a very hard break up. It was hard since he was still in school and was immature. I don't know the exact story either but his mom told me that they had to bring him far away from where he had lost himself. Now he'll walk out on you at some point and you both are going to end up hurt."

I locked myself up in my room that night scared and distorted. Tim barely spoke to me that evening. I came back alive when I saw his name on my mobile as he called.

"Hello?" I answered with panic.

"What's wrong?" he asked.

"I met Mitali in the evening."

"Oh, yeah right. I just got off the phone with her. What are you bothered about?" he asked in a soft voice, melting my fears.

"She warned me to stay away from you."

"It's alright. She cares about you."

"We're going to be fine, right?

"Why, yes sweetheart. Don't you worry now."

"I was scared." I cried out with relief. *"I can't imagine my life without you."* Tim remained calm. All I could hear was his balmy breath. *"You're not going to let me go, are you?"* his breathe faded and my heartbeat rose with its sound deafened. *"Tim?"*

"Shall we talk tomorrow?" he whispered, hesitantly.

"No." I screamed and then lowered my voice, afraid that my dad would hear me. *"No."* I repeated, with a sobbing

whisper.

"*Come on. Get to sleep. We shall talk tomorrow.*" I sunk onto my bed, and sobbed inconsolably. "*Trust me. Everything's going to be fine. Alright?*"

"*Ok.*"

He hung up the call without another word leaving me sleepless until early morning. I prayed that Tim wouldn't let go of me. I knew that he had a bad breakup which he wasn't over, though years passed by, and that he was afraid of getting into another relation, but I wished we could at least try.

The next morning, mom and dad noticed from my silence, that there was something wrong with me. "*You ok?*" dad questioned, looking at me peculiarly from over the table during breakfast.

"*I'm late.*" I lied. Dad turned his head and glanced at the wall clock on our side and then exchanged leery, mystified looks with mom. I hurried out, ignoring them and headed to my college. I couldn't wait to meet Tim and cling on to him as tightly as I could. I was only five minutes away from college and my mobile rang. I pulled it out of my handbag hastily, hoping it was Tim. The day seemed brighter, when I found out it was him and I answered without wasting any time.

"*Wanna bunk college and hang out?*" he asked, which struck my face with a smile. He didn't wait for me to answer. "*I'll come pick you up. Wait by the garden beside parking lot. I'm on my way.*"

"*Keep talking to me.*" I asked with an infantile sound.

"Ok, sweetie."

"How long will you take?"

"Soon."

I spoke to him for over ten minutes but the time seemed to have belittled. I was filled with a choppy feeling which made me turn my head to look behind me and Tim was creeping silently towards me. Giving up his cautious movement of approach, he let out a cunning laugh and walked to me. I was smitten with a potent urge to dash into him and grab him by his neck with my arms around him. Commanding myself not to over react, I walked to him and held his hand with a tight grip. For some strange reasons, I didn't long to ask Tim of our relationship. I was certain that he would make things right and never let me go. I had faith in him that he would make us work. We went out to the movies, then a drive and hung out at the coffee shop and I barely felt like I had to straighten out things with him.

"I'm not going to marry my daughter to you." My dad monished, when Tim dropped me home in the evening. Offended, Tim looked at my dad with a pinched face, forced a smile and replied straightforwardly,

"I never promised her of marriage. I sure love her, but I don't expect anything in return."

"Tim?" I called, alarmed. *"Dad?"*

"I wouldn't even dream of taking advantage on Saaya. You can trust me on this." Dad merely spoke on hearing Tim say that and I was shocked.

He walked away politely, with me glaring at my dad for being rude to Tim. *"I don't want you to be just another girl."*

143

He said, trying to endorsing himself. *"He never takes anything seriously.*

"He wouldn't let that happen to me." I guaranteed and walked briskly into my room.

I slid down onto thefloor, by the wall beside my bed, dialing Tim's number on my mobile. I waited for him to answer and,

"Yeah babe?" he answered, sounding as if nothing had happened.

"What was that?"

"What was what?"

"Your frigging statement about our marriage."

"Shall we talk about it tomorrow? In person? I would prefer not to have this conversation over a phone call."

"If you insist." I said, and hung up the call. Distressed and broke, I spent the rest of the night crying for a reason I didn't know. Late night on the same day, I wiped the tears off my face and cleared my eyes, as Tim called to my phone. I silenced myself and answered the call.

"Stop crying now." He hushed. I held the phone pressed closer to my ear and remained quiet. *"You look awful when you cry."* I wanted to tell him that I didn't want to lose him. All I could show him was my unfathomed pain. *"I promise that we shall talk tomorrow, alright?"*

"Do you really love me?" I questioned in a feeble whisper.

"We shall do this tomorrow. Sleep sweet now."

My mind was a bit ok after I spoke to Tim;I barely found any sleep that night.

I didn't carry my bag out of my bedroom the next morning before going to college.

"Where's your bag?" dad asked suspiciously.

"I'm not going to college today." I said, eating my breakfast. *"I want to get some clarifications from Tim, hopefully."*

"Evidently, he is not going to marry you."

"He said he's in love with me but never asked me if I did too. He's just not ready. If that is so, I want to hear it from him."

Dad dropped silent and continued eating his breakfast. Mom clasped her panic, worried if dad would burst out his anger. Except for the clinging sounds of forks and spoons, there was utmost silence at the table.I took dad's car and headed to café xo- the lounge bar in Govandi east, Mumbai. I reached well in advance to Tim and waited.Tim walked through the door hurriedly and eyed around for me, then eased up as he found me seated alone waiting for him.

"I'm sorry." He apologized. *"Bad traffic."*

"That's fine." I said, holding his hand as he sat next to me on the settee with a coffee table in our front.

"Did you order anything?"

"I had my breakfast."

"I'm hungry." He murmured as he went through the menu.

"Do you really love me?" I questioned.

145

"Of course I do." He answered, turning his head to look into my eyes.

"How do you intend to explain to me about yesterday?"

"I am certainly in love with you. I just haven't given our marriage a thought yet. What's the big deal?" he chuckled forcibly and fell back to a blank face.

"It's a big deal to me."

"Everything is going to be just fine. Trust me on this."

"I don't want this to be a passing by affair."

"It won't, alright? It won't. I'm just afraid that taking my damned past into consideration, your father wouldn't approve of our marriage. I have always been afraid of relationships and I'm afraid now too. I hope for this to work but I'm also scared that we're getting into something bigger than us. Let's take it slow."

"Love and marriage is not a game, Tim. It's not a relation which we can bargain upon. It's meant for the weak too, but we need to become strong from it."

"And how do you propose to do that?"

"We are going to be done with our engineering in few months. Crack a campus interview and get a joband the rest is my headache to make a wreak out of us." I critically explained, ordering his coffee, by pointing at the menu to the waiter.

"I won't lose you. I promise you that."

Tim took me shopping the day he introduced me to his parents as his girlfriend. We had fun with my being naughtier than ever. He had removed the cover of my silent nature by then. I must confess that I was never more with friends and family than I was alone.

Kosters didn't welcome me into their family. They treated me like I was born to them; me as their own daughter. It was fast but they accepted me wholeheartedly. But it wasn't the same with my father. He would not trust Tim so soon and Tim knew that. It gradually changed with Tim's multiple visits to my home every time he dropped me. Mom scorned at the sight of him that she would have had to break her promise because of him. Dad started liking him but trust didn't get in the way yet. Not until Kosters paid a formal visit and spoke about us. Mom had no choice but to forcibly agree to our marriage.

We had our first fight when Tim preferred to party with his friends rather than attending the campus interviews to grab a job. He was too careless while I was vexed that he didn't take things earnestly. *"I'll take something up. Don't worry."* He securely convinced me.

"You better start taking things seriously." I angered.

"I am not going to let anything mess up between us." He repeated.

"How?" I continued to express my anger in silent hardening tone so that dad wouldn't hear me fighting. *"When are you going to stop this sportive life?"*

"I will get a job before our marriage. Just stop worrying and have fun."

"We got to leave the fun aside for a while, Tim. You ought to know that."

It went on and one word led to another between us. Tim hung up the call frustrated and I forced myself to sleep.

I called him the next morning and he wouldn't answer. I got ready to college and hurried to meet him and make it up to him. His car was nowhere in the parking lot and I called to his mobile again. No answer. I continued calling him and saw his car drive in slowly. *"Why weren't you answering my calls?"* I questioned in an irritated voice.

"Shall we talk in the evening? I'm late for the class." He said, ignoring to look at me as he walked towards the classes.

"Since when did you start taking classes seriously?" I followed him. *"Speak up for God's sake. You're starting to make me think that I have made a tragic mistake."*

"We shall talk in the evening."

Giving up, I walked away. I was bothered by his denial to talk to me. I failed to concentrate on the classes. *"I'm sorry. Let us please skip the sessions in the noon and have lunch."* I sent him a message, discounting the lecture in the classroom. He didn't reply. I called him again during lunch break and he answered then. *"Tim I'm sorry."* I apologized.

"It's alright." He said.

"Please? Meet me at the parking lot. Lunch is on me."

He continued to carry the same serious face as he walked to me at the parking lot. *"Where to?"* he asked, opening the door to get behind the steering wheel. I squeezed myself in through the other door and gave him a hug, pulling him towards me.

"I'm sorry, alright?"

"Let it be. Where do you wanna go?" he asked.

*"Let us not get into conclusions."*I requested.

"We're good. I'll select the place. I have just the place in mind where you'll love the food." He smiled, started the car and drove.

Tim blended in, into our family and often joined us for family dinners. Dad would plan them, just to have Tim come over. Every time Kosters went shopping, they'd shower me with presents and surprises. Tim would deliver them to me at college sometimeswhich would lighten up my face."

#15

The evening grew darker as Saaya narrated their story. I could tell with absolute certainty that Saaya was still in love with Tim Koster. The sky was beaming with dropping sunlight on one side as the moon came up from the other. The expression on Anil's face was blank as earlier but Daphne put on, a sorrow pitiful expression for Saaya.

"Kosters spoke about our marriage with my parents and everything was falling in place." She continued. I turned into a pestering kind and Tim brushed aside his attention on me as long as he had to suppress his frustration. *"Would you please stop nagging?"* he would shout, hang up the phone and ignore me for a while. He's wily, I can give you that. Sometimes, afraid what our fight would turn into, I would decide not to call him unless he talked. He would call me back, start up the fight again, just so that he could talk to me." Saaya laughed to herself, forcibly. "Fights I had with him are pretty funny to me now. His cunning arrogance makes me laugh.Every day was a time travel to the previous day. I shifted back to the same love and care, and fights every day. I certainly didn't grow old on him. My dreams were only growing bigger when he proposed to me to marry him.

"*Saaya Viroodh? Will you marry me and make me the luckiest person on earth?*" he proposed, looking up at me and hoisting to me, a shiny beautiful ring with his fingers. I stood there, my jaw dropped, tears fighting their way to get out. It was out of the blue with all my friends around me at a coffee shop.

"*Yes.*" I said with a very low indistinct voice. "*Definitely yes.*" I pulled him onto his feet forcibly and hugged him as tight as I could. Breaking away from me gently as if I were so delicate, he wore the ring to my finger. I was too preoccupied by that breathtaking excitement.

That was one of the most memorable days in my life and it ended with a dinner with Tim's parents. Tim Koster was not just a great guy. He was fun, always full of surprises. He could make me feel a hundred things at a time. He could make me smile right after a silent cry. He could make me laugh with tears right after a childish fight. He could make me fall in love with him a thousand times. He always kept me amused and made me wonder what was in store for us.

The next morning, mom popped up an argument and started being a little captious with Tim.

"*He's not determined enough.*" She complained. "*I hope he could be a little more responsible and get a job.*"

"*He knows how to take care of our daughter and keep her happy. I find no reason for us to be worried.*" Dad supported.

"*Bye dad.*" I got up from the table with unfinished breakfast and left giving mom a disapproving look.

I was afraid to bring up with Tim the topic about his getting a job. I was afraid that it would only lead to another fight. Fears dropped my happiness like a sack of potatoes. Words of love and care subsided as days passed. Tim was consecrated enough with me to notice my silence. He tried talking me out of it but we only ended up arguing. He felt hurt with my calling him undetermined and irresponsible one evening after college.

"*What on earth made you say that?*" he questioned vexed up.

"*You.*" I screamed back. "*It will be a lot better if you take things seriously. I insist.*"

"*Oh, now I'm just killing time with you? Is that what you're trying to say?*" he angered, getting into his car.

"*Go ahead. Show your ego and walk away like you always do. Have fun running away from life.*"

"*I'm frigging livin' it. And I'm livin' it with you no matter what. I don't see why you keep doing this all the time.*"

"*I want you to stop living off your dad's money and shoulder some responsibility.*" I continued to scream.

"*How come you never mentioned that in the beginning? Did it take you four years to realize that I'm irresponsible?*" he shouted at the top of the voice.

"*Yes.*" I answered sternly. "*I hope I had realized that earlier. I'm such a chicken to drag myself behind you all the time. I can't take your arrogance anymore.*"

"*I wasn't the one who started all this.*" He shouted.

"*Neither did I.*" I argued absent mindedly. "*I should*

152

have listened to my mother."

"To hell. I never pushed you into marriage. You were the one who dropped me into this" He shouted, his face going red in color.

"Now you're telling me that I forced you into all of this?" I squealed, angrily, deeply hurt.

"Yes." He shouted. *"I never wanted to get into this. You dragged into it and made this complicated. I regret talking to you in the first place. I should have held back my love for you. I shouldn't have let it out in the open."*

"You're free, Tim Koster. You can walk away, and keep your bloody love to yourself and dust your hands off of all this. As for me, I can never be happy with you anymore. I can't put my life in your hands and suffer with your arrogance. It freaks me out to think how and when, you would react to what. I cannot live a frightened life with you." I screamed at the top of my voice. He stood there for half a minute, looking at my reddened face, and jumped into his car with a rage. I got into mine and drove home.

It didn't take my wrath, much of a time to hate Tim and talk mom into my marrying my cousin. *"Are you sure about this?"* dad asked as mom readily made calls for the engagement.

"Yes, dad." I answered. *"He's still the same old fun loving spoilt brat. I was wrong about him that he had turned serious with his life and me. I can't be happy with him anymore. I want my own life. He's better off without me."*

I never saw Tim after that. I didn't call him anymore. I prevented myself from talking to him. It was hard, but I was determined to do it. I convinced and cheated myself that

I could live without him. I developed a strong urge to prepare myself to be happily married to my cousin. Mom made arrangements with the speed of a lightning bolt afraid that I would change my mind. I remained hidden from all our mutual friends during my engagement. I didn't want to be messed up about this topic. I was filled with a deep feeling that I deserved a better life of my own. I made sure not many were invited for my engagement. I wanted to lay it low and finish it. I turned my mobile off that Tim was continuously calling me. Regardless of my attempts to silently get engaged, he turned up and showed his rage. He met with an accident later and when I heard, I was worried, and broke. I let a breath out when my friends told me that he was alive. I killed my feelings for him. I couldn't show them out to anyone. When Tim appeared at my wedding, I was puzzled. I felt it heavily impossible to read his mind. His face was blank and it was as if he was blocking me from his heart. I wanted to get up and go to him, but it was too late by then. I should say that I had never fallen in love with him. His love drew me towards him. I can never forgive myself for making him watch my wedding. Not after I knew how much he loved me.

I wish I had the capability to realize my mistakes a lot earlier. Everyone imagines me to be married and happy, but they can never look through my eyes. No one can feel my pain that's dissolved deep inside me. Apparently, I can't let my blunder affect my husband. He married me and I can't hurt him with my past. I need to let my past go. I only wish that I could live a life someday, rather than continue pretending it."

#16

Saaya finished and stayed calm. Took a very long pause. Probably all the memories started to flash in her mind. I turned my eyes away from her and at the darkened sky. Daphne took Saaya downstairs and we spent a little longer with her. On our way back home, Saaya's story was all that I could either think or dream of. My shoulder had gone numb at Daphne's sleepy head on it. Her hair that fell on my arms didn't tickle. Anil's swerving the car or sudden apply of the brakes didn't startle me. My mind was hovering over Tim and Saaya's love. I could feel the hunger for a story, addicted, curious and greed. That was the true construct of their story. Daphne woke up from the sound sleep and lifted her head up from my shoulder as Anil brought the car to a sudden halt, at reaching home.

"Tim?" I heard Daphne's muffled voice from deep in my head. I prompted my mind back to reality and, "Vian?" I heard again.

155

"Vian!" she called again to draw my attention, doubtfully looking at me with her tired sleepy eyes.

"Yeah." I sighed, and turned to see our home through the window. I pulled out my mobile as we walked in, and noticed Uncle Jamie's missed calls. He had called me five times that evening. I thought to myself. "Was I so much indulged into the story?"

"I'm sorry Uncle Jamie, I missed your calls." I spoke over the phone as he answered.

"That's alright. I have called to know if you have completed the story. I spoke to my team about it." He finished.

"It's almost done." I answered in a lowered tone.

"Vian. We have a schedule to follow."

"The story is complete, but I couldn't find a perfect ending yet." I tried to explain.

"Sit on it tonight, finish the story, and send me something by tomorrow." He continued. "You will do well. Just trust yourself. Give it your best shot."

I dropped down on the couch like a bird with a broken wing and descended into deeper thoughts. I couldn't just end Tim and Saaya's story with their egoistic confrontations and a breakup. I didn't want it to end up as a pitiful, sad, unfortunate story.

"What's the matter?" Daphne leaped beside me on the couch and grabbed me by my arm.

"Uncle Jamie wants the story tomorrow. I have a

deadline." I spoke unconfidently.

"That's great news. Why's that keeping you worried?" she questioned, caressing the back of my palm with her cold hands.

"I still don't have Tim's story." I groaned.

"He's a hard one to find. He wouldn't even bother talking. You got the story anyway. Work on it. I'll stay awake with you."

"Yeah, will do." I agreed and wandered back into my thoughts. Love is not just a feeling to express. Love is losing control of body and soul. Love is jumping to different worlds and diving into thickest dreams. Although Tim Koster's existence remained a mere mystery, I concluded the story in short with a notional ending, making it look like a fiction and emailed it to Uncle Jamie along with submission components such as the pitch of the story, synopsis, sample chapters, etc. Uncle Jamie said he would call me with the review and their decision. He warned me beforehand that there were only one percent chances that they'd accept my novel. My running errands for digging out the story came to an end and it was time for us to rejoice Mitali and Ryna's wedding ceremony.

Tiresome shopping throughout the day, hanging out in the evenings and night, dinners at Daphne's home, went by leaving a spark of splendid memories in my mind.

"My mom likes you a lot." Daphne said while we were shopping ornaments for Mitali one day along with Ryna's parents.

"Mmhmm?"

"Yeah. Last night we were having a casual talk after dinner and she told me that you were so sweet."

"Glad to know." I replied. Ryna and Mitali weren't supposed to stay away from their respective homes until wedding date according to Indian tradition. So the remaining of us occupied my parents' home until the date. Tony and Lisa arrived a few days before. For a few weeks, our home was filled with lot; fun, laughter, crazy chit chatting, delicious Indian food, secret crush talks, mom and dad's love story, et cetera. I had no idea about the others but my stomach definitely ached every night before I went to sleep due to the heavy laughter.

Mitali and Ryna'swedding was a blast and a gracious event in all of our lives. It was a heavenly feeling to see every single one of them shed tears with immense happiness and joy. Mitali's dad cried like a child out of pride and joy after all the guests had left. "I'm so proud of you." He let out a squeezed whisper as Mitali clung onto him like a small baby girl.Her face was well lit by the decoration lights falling through the darkness of the night.

"How did the wedding go?" Uncle Jamie asked over the phone as I walked away from the noise so I could hear him.

"Awesome." I answered.

"Had fun?"

"Yeah. A lot."

"I have something else for you. We are going to publish your novel. Schedule your travel as soon as possible to come sign the contract." He finished. I didn't utter a word but stood stunned and petrified. I felt like I went into a concussion as if it were all a dream. "The editorial team will be sending you an official email or call you later today evening but I wanted to break it out to you myself."

"I, uh- I don't know what to say." I stuttered, with a feeling of punctured nerves on my hands.

"I get it. Go celebrate. Give my love to mom and dad, and congratulate the newly wedded couple on my behalf."

"Will do. Thank you very much Uncle Jamie."

"What is it?" Daphne questioned puzzled and worried, as I walked back to them.

"They're going to sign me up." I blabbered delightfully.

"No way. You're kidding." Mitali exclaimed breaking herself free from her dad.

"Why would I?"

Daphne threw herself onto me and tangled my neck with her arms, slightly pushing me backwards. Mitali and Ryna fell onto me behind Daphne and choked me out of breath.

"I'm proud of you." My dad muttered with triumph as I walked slowly into his arms. I rested my chin on his shoulder and began to cry. "Now there's the girl in you." He teased. I could feel mom from behind me kissing the back of my head and running her palms over my hair, but I gripped dad so tight and continued to weep silently.

Mitali and Ryna got busy getting habituated and rejoicing a life together while I planned my travel back to

New York with Tony and Lisa. I would be coming back to India after my master's program. It was the first time ever when mom hadn't cried while seeing me off at the airport. I could see the pride and tears of glory in her eyes.

"Come back soon." Daphne whispered silently smiling through her glittering eyes. "I'm going to miss you." I gave her a gentle hug and walked away for checking in.

Lisa was seated between Tony and me in the plane and we had fun teasing her. She argued with us on every single matter like a child, trying to pull our legs.

"You didn't tell us that she is this irrational." I teased, talking to Tony and he broke into a laugh. "You told me she was silent."

"Asshole!" Lisa called out hitting on my shoulder as we laughed at her. "I'm not gonna talk anymore."

"That's highly impossible." Tony countered. Lisa didn't rest her mouth all the way long. She was talking, talking and talking. It was so sweet to watch her talk to me and Tony and the chemistry of love and care between them.

I wasn't tired of the travel. The funny, amusing conversation and arguments we had kept me highly entertained. I hired a cab to my apartment from the airport after we reached and Tony and Lisa left to their home. I was very much excited about the story, but what happened of Tim Koster, remained a mystery. I was reluctant to get the story published with an inappropriately carved up ending but there was nothing I could do to make it better without laying my ears upon the truth. It seemed like smoke without a fire. Later at my apartment, I stood under the shower, cooling my head off with white fumes emerging out of my body as I thought of any possible modifications in the story. It's now a fiction anyway. I then finally decided that it was good to go, and got dressed into my night robes and hit the lights out before I crashed onto my bed for a sound sleep.

#17

The next morning, Uncle Jamie called me on my mobile to confirm if I have received the contract documents they emailed. I checked my inbox through my mobile phone.

"Yeah I got the email." I said.

"We will forward the manuscript to the printing department once we receive the signed documents. I'm kind of in a hurry now. Please go through the terms and conditions very carefully before signing."

"Thank you. I will look into it." I said.

"What about Ryna? When's he coming? You guys have final semester exams, don't you?"

"They'll be back New York in the next few days before the exams. They have some traditions to get the whole wedding thing over with."

After I got off the phone with Uncle Jamie, I sat at my desk and went through the manuscript in the evening through the night. No matter how hard I thought, I failed to come up with any idea or modification. The cursor on the screen automatically crawled to a folder on my desktop which contained Tianna's pictures and I opened it with a huge hesitation. Giving half a minute's thinking, I reluctantly clicked on her pictures and viewed them; memories of our old times when we were together. I let out a heavy silent breath and, 'Lose them, Vian.' I spoke to myself. 'Just lose them.' I clicked on the folder to select it, pressed shift plus delete and then stared blankly at the warning on the screen, *"Are you sure you want to permanently delete this folder?"* I gathered all my courage and clicked, *'Yes.'* I snubbed my decision of getting rid of her pictures. Nonetheless, I was in the spur of the moment and erased all her memories, once and for all.

I wanted to wait until I finished my exams to sign the contract. My mind was free of disarrays finally that I had done an impressive and successful work with Tim Koster's story. I was worried if he would object my getting his story published; but since his parents approved of it, and I wrote it more like a fiction instead of his biography, I settled my mind conclusively to go ahead. I made a terrible performance in my exams along with Ryna and I was excited that I had completed my Master's program, somehow. I was suddenly reminded of my neighbors back in India. He was married with two kids and a well settled business man. His elder son who had finished his twelfth grade then, got a phrase stickered on the rear window of his dad's car, just for the fun of it. *"I have to pass tenth grade somehow.'* It read. Uncle's wife read it along with their two sons and laughed until their tummies ached one morning. I noticed them from my balcony and when I asked what it was about, she told me with great difficulty as she continued to laugh. "Uncle failed his tenth thrice and dropped out of school."

"Get a mike and tell the whole town." Uncle sarcastically teased and went back inside.

I now somehow completed my education. My face had a smile imprinted all the while and I was no more worried about anything. After my final exam, Ryna, Mitali, Tony, Lisa and I had dinner at a restaurant where we had fun filled with laughter and loving moments. I headed to my apartment late night alone, later after the dinner. With my friends getting busier day by day with their married life and career, all I could take along with me were their memories. Reaching home, I placed my car keys in a tray on my desk and walked in reloading email inbox in my phone. I planned to sign and send back the contract, first thing in the morning the next day. I would then spend a few weeks in US and return to India. Dad would sell my apartment and have their house rented or would either put it for sale. Mom wanted me to take up some business in India and marry an Indian girl. They could never ask for more of me and I was determined to fulfill their wish. Drifting into a sound sleep wasn't a problem anymore. No memories were spine-chilling to haunt me in my dreams either. I managed to fall asleep that night without dragging any time and effort.

Next day, at 12 in the noon, I was rushing to the airport, and waited for a cab down my apartment when I called Uncle Jamie. "You done?" he asked as soon as he answered.

"I need more time." I answered afraid that he would be mad at me.

"But we have already sent you the contract."

"Yes, the story is not complete. I want the story to be perfect."

"Do you realize what you are doing? This window will close up on you once you walk past it."

"Yes, but if the story is not right, what's the whole point?This is my last and final attempt to find out the exact story of Tim Koster. An incomplete story is in fact not a story at all."

He remained calm for a while and, "Go get it then. Finish what you started." He encouraged.

"Jamie! You're my man. I love you." It's been ages since I called him by his name. When I was full grown kid, I used to call him by his name just to tease him. I used to imitate how my mom and dad called him.

"Take care." He softly said.

I jumped into a cab, recollecting what had happened, early that morning.

I was awakened to the loud vibrating of my mobile on the desk beside my bed early in the morning in the resting silence of the city. It was an unknown Indian number. Wondering if it was Daphne, I answered with a lazy grunting voice. "Vian Bansi!"

"I'm sorry if I wokeyou up too early." A manly voice spoke. It wasn't entirely soft and not exactly harsh either.

"That's alright. May I know who this is?"

"Tim Koster!" the voice said. The sound of it, opened up my eyes wide enough that I felt the eyelids were going to split apart and that I was shaken from a hundred-year long sleep like that of a vampire. I almost choked out. I didn't know what to say I was curious, I was shocked, I was excited. I was feeling at least ten entirely different things."Vian?" he called again.

"Yes. Yes." I stammered. "Tim! Hey! This is so embarrassing. I'm just surprised. I didn't see this coming."

"I understand. I'm sorry to bother but I just heard from my parents and wanted to give you a call."

"I'm really glad you called. It's- I might take a while to let this call soak in, man."

"No problem. Are you still in India? Can we meet? I just want to do some catching up just so you don't place any rumors which you might have heard, in your novel."

"Sure. I'm still in India." I lied."Name the place. I'll be there." I agreed.

"Dublin pub, New Delhi, Friday after 6 PM? It's a perfect place to hang out. I'm a regular there."

"Terrific! I will be there." I readily confirmed. "I'll email you the story I drafted so far. You can go through if you have time. Can I have your email id?"

"I'll text you my id. See you on Friday then. I heard a lot about you and would like to listen to your story too."

I chuckled as he dropped the call and sat up on my bed wondering if that was a dream. "Did you talk to Mitali?"

"I'll call her. I missed her wedding. She is probably mad at me by now. I'll make it up to her when I next meet her."

"Ok. She was worried a lot."

"Yeah. Shouldn't have disappeared like that, but I badly needed some time."

"I understand."

"Alright. See you on Friday."

"Sure." I said and hung up. I placed my mobile back on the bedside table and lied flat, wondering if it was all just a dream. I badly wanted to know what happened next. I wanted to hear Tim's story. I just couldn't wait. With an abrupt move, I grabbed my phone to check for the available flights to New Delhi while I packed my bag with clothes and stuff. I then snatched a towel and rushed into the bathroom to take a shower. I later called Uncle Jamie and then got into the cab to the airport. Luckily there was a flight available for the afternoon. I was struck with mixed feelings about Tim Koster. His voice depicted the most formal tone of a perfect gentleman. His tone failed to carry any sign of fun and happiness in his life. Fun, laughter, luxuries are what we call a life? No! Life is a bitch. When we fight back against the pain it gives us, ignore all the crap it dips us in and get through the hassles it causes, that's what we call, living a life. Most importantly, Tim Koster was alive. I could sense the dreams turn to reality. The nightmares seemed to fade with time as I sat in the plane to New Delhi. It was time for me to last my juvenile cries and move on with my life. I had a feeling in my gut, that this was going to change me in some way. I wondered what God has in store for me.

With the perfect turning of events, life to me appeared beautiful all of a sudden. I enjoyed the food and coffee served in the plane as I waited for it to land in New Delhi. I know, that meeting Tim couldn't probably be one of the life events. But given the last few trips to India and all the digging for the story, I was excited as hell to meet him.I called Daphne as soon as I hired a cab to a hotel in Delhi on Friday morning after reaching. I spoke to mom and dad later over the phone for about half an hour and promised them that I'd pay them a visit before I return to New York. I passed on Tim's mobile number to Mitali and Ryna as I settled my luggage on the bed in the hotel. I took a quick shower and then took a daylight nap. I ordered a coffee somewhere at 4 PM and drowsily walked into the bathroom to take a shower again. I rushed out wrapping up a towel around my waist as I heard my phone ring from outside the bathroom, imagining it was Tim. I took it up from over the bed with my wet hands and it was Daphne.

"When are you coming to Mumbai?" she asked, excitedly. "Mitali just called. She spoke to Tim."

"In a few days, maybe."

"Really?"

"Yeah babe."

"Did you meet Koster yet?"

"I'm meeting him at 6."

"Tell him I said hi. You take care now."

"Yeah you too."

#18

I wiped the wet off the phone that it had caught from my drenched head from the shower, to my towel, tossed it onto the bed and slid into a pair of clothes. Hurrying out of the hotel, I waited for a cab and it was 5 PM by the hands of my watch. I waved my hand when I saw a cab drive towards me and got in. I sat there in the rear seat, thinking. It took me a year to find Tim Koster. I had never met this guy and I only spoke to him for just a few minutes over the phone but I so felt like I knew him all along. I was concerned about what shape I was going to find Tim in. I was worried how broken the poor guy would be. With him losing his love, he probably would be getting drunk in the bar and going back home, everyday.I could imagine the pain he would savor. I had been there after Tianna dumped me. Saaya getting married would have had hit him like burning a hole in his bleeding heart. I stepped out of the cab observing the surroundings as I reached the pub and dialed to Tim's phone. I waited for him to answer my call but he didn't. I rang him thrice and went in by myself. My memory flashed back to the time when I first met Mitali at Fontana's.

The deafening Indian remix music was a celebration beat. I searched for Tim Koster in the flashing disco lights, although I didn't have a clear picture of his face in my mind. It had been a very long time since I checked his pictures on Facebook. I walked over to a bouncer standing stiff by the dance floor and,

"Hey! By any chance, do you happen to know Tim Koster?" I asked. He pointed his finger towards the bar counter where there were two guys drinking crazy as hell. The one in red t-shirt was sitting on a chair, with his back facing me and his face turned to his side looking at the other guy. He bore a saddened expression on his face listening to the other guy in black who was cheering and pushing him with the drinks. Just as I had expected, Tim Koster was broken and stuck in his past with his friend jollying him up. No wonder he ran away so far from home to hide his mourning face that rained with dark sorrows. No wonder he had gone into a hiding from all his loved ones to save him the embarrassment of losing his love. "The guy in the red, right?"

"No. Guy in the black." The bouncer shouted through the loud music around, with a hard tone and bearing no expression on his face. I twisted my head to look at the bouncer with surprise and he wasn't kidding. I turned back slowly towards those two guys and eyed the guy in the black, Tim Koster. Of course it was him; lively, happy, resilient, and rejoicing. It took me so long to find Tim Koster and he wasn't exactly what I had expected him to be. He was right there in front of my eyes, having a really good evening, in the pub, like a man freed from a life sentence. I had imagined him to be drenched with tears but his face seemed to illuminate with victory. Should I have been glad that he was doing ok? Or should I have been disappointed that he was entirely different from what I had imagined him to be. As I walked petrified towards him, the reasoned train of my thoughts on him of the grief from his loss, began to change completely. I suspected that he wasn't truly in love at all to begin with. I wondered if Saaya was just another number.

"Vian Bansi!" I choked out, giving my hand to him for a shake.

Noticing me, "Hey! So you made it." he exclaimed, shaking my hand and gave me a gentle hug. "I'm really sorry! Did you call? I forgot my mobile in my car."

"Yes, but it wasn't hard finding you." Tim nodded to the bartender to fix me a drink and while he was at it,

"Oh! Hah. I'm a regular here." He chuckled.

"Figured."

"I've read your story. That's quite an impressive work you've done. You didn't walk the story off the right track."

"I imagined you to be more of a-" I started, looking puzzled at him.

"What, like lonely, sad and alcoholic?" he chuckled. "Vian! This is Sam, my friend and colleague from my work place, Sam! This is Vian Bansi." He introduced.

"What happened to you?" I questioned, unable to loosen the astonishment.

"I'm not sure I'm following you." He gestured for me to repeat the question in an understandable way.

"After the breakup; after Saaya got married, what

171

happened? How in the world do you manage to be so calm? Did you find someone else who mended you?"

"Falling in love twice, is like falling out of a frying pan and running into the fire. But yes; I fell in love." He answered sternly. "I fell in love again after she got married."

"Shocking!" I commented. "With whom?"

"With myself." He countered. "I got busy with my life and more often made sure I was preoccupied. If you wouldn't fall in love with yourself, Vian, you're missing the greatest feeling in your life."

"Hmm." I made a sound, finding it hard to talk.

"Shall we get out? Let's get some air." He suggested.

"Sure thing." I agreed and he picked up his jacket from the chair beside him.

"You guys go ahead. I will join the others." Sam bailed out.

"So, how's life treating you?" Tim asked me as we walked out of the pub to his car.

"How did you fall in love?" I asked at once.

"Well, there's a lot of love out there in the world. Even if you don't want it, it's going to hit you right in the face. Well, it hit me too, but ended up breaking me apart."

"What happened with Gargi and Asna?" I questioned.

"I don't want to get into conclusions about Gargi. I would prefer to let it be. I didn't want to be with someone who couldn't value relations. So when I learnt of Sean, I broke up with her. Sean was a very good guy and in no way I intended to steal his girl from him. I hope she didn't blow another chance he had given to her later. Asna was cool, but we didn't get along that well. We were better off as friends. I mean I sure had feelings for her in the beginning since she's sweet, but then I realized that her dad would never agree for a love marriage so we didn't even get there."

"What happened with Saaya?"

"That's lot of questions, Vian. Straight on to my face." He joked.

"I'm sorry. I've been asking these questions for a very long time in my head. Now that I found you, I'm unable to handle my curiosity. That's the problem with writers. When we see a story, we need to know."

"I didn't just take her in. I seriously do not know how or why I fell in love. It just, happened. She was my face of the truth."

"I would still ask; how did that happen?"

"I was entirely blindfolded on how and when it happened. I failed to notice that she was running in my mind. When I first saw her while we were ragging our juniors during our second year, I was so lost that I let Saaya and her friend go.I was struck by an unknown feeling which I was sure would never perish. I felt that not thinking about her was hard. Her beautiful face was beyond the power of my imagination. My moment had begun where my feeling for her was greater than my willpower and I was not to be trusted with myself. In every way, I retained myself from talking to her. There was a glitch in my past. High school love, she ditched me and I couldn't take it. I mean I was born and brought up in a western culture but there's still that Indian blood which triggers our feelings meaninglessly. I was afraid of relationships since then and walked away on a few, later. I was afraid I wouldn't be able to take Saaya seriously. Saaya was sweet and I wasn't the right one for someone so good.It was the sign of fortune that she passed by me every single day at college making it a punishing task for me to ignore. Her way of displaying her fears towards me, made me decide not to bother her by any means. I felt that she would be far safer without me. Yet one evening, she stood alone during a fresher's party, watching the programs on stage. I was loitering around, checking up on the arrangements and she turned her head to the ground at the sight of my walking towards her. I approached her, and,

"*Something wrong with the ground?*" I tried to cheer her up. "*You can look up and have fun. Do not worry about anything.*"

"*I tend to remain scared in the beginning.*" She spoke with an innocently lowered tone.

"*Everyone is very friendly; you can be free, turn to any of us for help. We don't treat you people as lunch and we're definitely not hungry.*" I went on and she asked me for my number which made me feel, so happy. I readily exchanged numbers with her, spoke to her for a while and left. I began to see the end of windings in my life. She was an inevitable moment in my life."

#19

"You had yourself drowned neck deep in love for her by then, I guess?"

"You could say that." He agreed. "Love is a strange thing, Vian. You never know where it comes from and how, but it hits you so hard and you don't feel a thing until you lose it. I bunked my classes and was hanging out with Nevan and others when Saaya sent me the first text calling for help. I just, dashed away towards her lab and found some third year guy trying to be sweet and all, making her uncomfortable. I walked her to the lab from him.I should actually thank him since Saaya spoke to me because of him. As expected, it hurt the seniors' ego. They cornered me a couple of times when I was alone."

"Couple of times?" I interrupted. "I thought it was just once."

"Nah. I did take a beating more than once man. I

couldn't shake them all off, alone on my own.Vincent was the one who had my back. Without him, I wouldn't be sitting with you here in one piece.We can never repay someone who helps us wholeheartedly in a better way than with gratitude. Our entire life can never suffice such a helping hand.No matter how many times I tried to keep away from Saaya, I was drawn towards her. I learnt from her, the true value of love. I spent more time with my parents then and realized how happy my mom could be from a loving kiss from me every day. Did you ever feel like the air that you breathe out, gets stuck in your throat with, uh, how do I say that, umm, delectation?"

"Uh hmm, not exactly." I answered and listened to him keenly with extreme admiration.

"I had that feeling like a hundred times. Every time Saaya told me that she loved me, or surprised me, and better yet, when I showed how much I loved my mom and dad, and the smile they shot at me. I never was aware until then, how much pleasure it gives us to give happiness for the people we love. Everyone looked upon Saaya as an innocent girl but she was brave as hell. She's my sweetest nightmare." Tim went on as we got into his car and drove out of the parking lot. "It was my mistake; entirely. Girls, are a sensitive kind. No matter how strong a girl is, she's sure as hell to be deranged due to some problem which she could never express. Saaya was sensitive too; soft, delicate and vulnerable. I shouldn't have been so hard on her. I should have tried talking her out. I should have sunk her provocation with love and care. I shouldn't have added heat to her burning mind. I should have understood that she was in fact fighting with me for us to be together. I should have realized that she was fighting with me, for me. I should have let our love win, over my arrogance. I was blind upon the love she shed over me. If it wasn't for my snobbery ego, she would be living a blissful and happiest life with me now; a joyful life, rather than simply leading a life without me. However, I'm a bit mad at her, for breaking up with me that way. I failed to convince her wrong of her stubbornness.The least she could have done was to at least listen to my apology. She froze her mind from me. I wanted to hate her for doing that to me, but I loved her. I loved her enough to forget her and be happy since that is what she would want me to do."

"What happened after the accident?" I asked, gazing at him as he narrated.

"All along as I tried apologizing and convincing Saaya. I tried calling her but she was already determined and turned her mobile off. I was too late to hold her hands and plead her to come back to me. She was already engaged by the time I reached her home after I heard the sudden news. After I woke up from the hospital, I just left. I made contact with a friend of mine in Delhi, and then travelled with most of my body wrapped up in bandages and my hand dressed with plaster of Paris. I didn't know what to do. I couldn't think or decide upon anything. All I wanted was to go as far as I could from her. It took me about two months to be healed of all my physical injuries. That excruciating phase made me forget all other people who loved me, including my parents. I didn't have the nerve to face anyone.I was mad, angry, and furious, and all the same, I wanted to invoke her to come back to me. Saaya was the only one who could save me from that kind of a situation but she abandoned me. I was helpless. There was nothing I could do. I realized that I had to live with it.

I wondered how, she could choose to be so happy

177

while I suffered. I don't know the view of perspective of everybody else but according to me, a girl regards the guy, as the guys she falls in love with, whom she could never live without; and whom she would want to share her life with. A man looks at his girl, as a child, someone he needs to take care of, someone he should keep happy all the time. Love has so much power that it makes us see faces in thin air. It prevents us from sorrows and pain, but the moment the love is gone and the cover is blown, nothing else can protect us from being broken and hurt. I didn't understand whence all of that came. I spent biding my time alone stuck in her memories. I couldn't sleep and even if I did manage to fall asleep, I often felt shaken up with nightmares. I turned into a coward. I was afraid all the time. I was far away from feeling numb. I went on rash drives to suppress my anger and pain. I woke up every single morning to realize that she was no more in my life. I fell asleep on her infliction every night. I wanted to look back and remember the moments I spent with her but all I could do was pine for her. Sweetest memories turned into horrible nightmares. Reality turned fantasy, I lost track of my life. I got wasted every night in bars and got into a couple of fights. Finding stability to my mind was an impossible task.I thought that girls knew all manner of escape contrives. But then, I had a part in it too. Love is a mere overture to suffering. Blinded by agony she caused, I failed to notice the signs of warning of life.

I don't blame her though. Her mistake was my responsibility. My friends were against me getting into Saaya's life, for they feared that I might walk out on her. They told me that she was too good for me to hold on to.To begin with I had no intention to get into a relationship with her or marry her or lead a life with her. I wouldn't call it love if I wanted to own her. She's not just some, thing man. We are people with feelings and emotions. I was in love. The only desire I had was for her to be happy no matter where she was. I couldn't abandon her either. I felt that she was better off without me. I was afraid to face her. I was unsure of how to talk to her. I tried to ignore her but that only made things worse. When she came home and held on to me tight, I was proved wrong. It didn't matter what people thoughtabout us. It's what and who we were, and what was between us that really counted most. I could read the happiness in her eyes when I'm with her. I could see her dream of me. I wanted to make it real for her. My mood swings started hitting up as I grew worried about her day by day. I wished that I could quit talking to her for a while until I fixed things up for us.But later, I needed so much pain to uphold my breakaway from her.

It was at times slippery. I used my anger to seize my life back to normal. I was under the misapprehension that I would not be able to wrap it up and be happy again. I was worried about how I could end up when I was alone, without her. I was bleary all the time and I could not find any sleep. I found a job and I was a slowpoke at work in the beginning but I started catching up. I made good friends and hung out often with them for a change. I retained the fun I could have had. I was glad with my caution to act. I struggled to free myself from my heinous past. I pushed myself into the conversations of my colleagues and maintained a very good reputation which bought me quite a lot of pals.The changes I have made in my life seemed impressive to me. How difficult it was to forget her and yet how important to live with her memories. I was an architect of my own life. Everybody is to their own. It might have been easy for her to accept somebody else, but I was destined to go through a wretched time. I had to go through a lot of obstacles but believe me when I tell you, that there are millions more who took a lot worse blows than I did. I may have cried for her every night, but come daylight, I started living a life for myself, for the people left in my life and who loved me.

I still have her voice running in my head." He forced a smile to cover up his sadness. *"I can never be happy with you anymore. I can't put my life in your hands and suffer with your arrogance. It freaks me out to think how, you would react to what. I cannot live a frightened life with you."* I thought she loved me and that she couldn't live without me."

I went on listening to his distressed story as I sat beside him. He paused for a while to catch up some breath and control his emotions. I could see his lips tremble with nervousness. He tapped his fingers on the steering wheel. "You don't have to do this if you're feeling uncomfortable." I gave in.

"Oh! No, no no. It's alright. I've been through worse. Heh he." He chuckled forcibly and right away put a blank face, as he lost himself in his thoughts. He wet his lips and, "She was worth taking a bruise; worth all the pain." He went on. "I hid here in Delhi, taking out my frustration on punching boxing bags and furious drives. I reached a point where I wanted to die. I wished Saaya was there to make me lose the pain but she wasn't anymore. I got a call from Mr. Viroodh. He contacted me through an email and I gave him my number.

"Tim?" he called, as I answered.

"How are you, uncle?"

"How are you Tim? Where have you been?"

"I'm in Delhi."

"*Why did you give up on Saaya, Tim?*"

"*I don't recall Saaya being any too certain about us getting married.*" I answered. "*And you couldn't stop her from walking away from me, could you?*"

"*I don't want to prolong this conversation.*" He said in a lowered tone.

"*What happened to her?*" I asked him worriedly.

"*She's marrying her cousin.*"

"*Just as she wanted it to be.*"

"*She doesn't know what she's doing, Tim. She's marrying someone she doesn't love and it's going to be too late by the time she realizes it. She'll look back and find out that she has already walked away from you. I don't want my daughter to be disappointed.*" He said. I could sense his concern for the both of us. I didn't know what to say. I didn't realize that I was too arrogant to ask him for his help.

"*There's nothing I can do now. It's way out of my hands.*" I denied. "*I don't want her to change her mind again. I want her to be happy.*"

"*Give yourself one last chance.*"he said and hung up. Probably, he got tired of trying to explaining to me too. That was how I was. Blind." He stared straight at the road, with regret in his eyes.

#20

"I accepted his invitation to his daughter's wedding and flew to Mumbai. I traveled with hesitation. I was afraid to face the weakness of my falling in love with her all over again. I was certain of her being strong with her decision no matter what. I wanted to be stronger than that. I wished that I could look her straight in the eye, and walk away without any emotional feeling. I hired a cab from the airport and went home. I was afraid of facing my parents too, since I was away from them for a long time. I only spoke to them over the phone and didn't let them come visit me; asked them not to let anyone know my whereabouts. I just wanted some time for myself.After the cab pulled by the gate to my home, I remained seated in it for about five minutes, worried how they would react. I took a deep breath in and got out, paying the fare. I walked in through the gate and past the garden very slowly. I then stood by the door, and my mom froze at the sight of me. My dad was sitting on a couch, noticed her and then turned to me. He almost jumped off the couch, came to me and hugged me with his hefty arms. I could see how worried they were about me. I didn't even give them a chance to be with me when I was going through a rough phase. Mom walked towards me in utmost bewilderment as if she couldn't believe her eyes, and I broke free from dad to hug her. She held me by the sides of my face with her cold palms and looked into my eyes, crying. Mothers, right? We take them for sentimental fools but would we ever be able to find anyone who could love us like a mother?

"I'm sorry ma!" I apologized. I sat there silently, holding onto them, regretting for what I've done. How did I miss them? I could see the anger in my parents' love that I deserted. I could see the pain they went through in the tears they shed at the sight of me.

"You must be hungry. I'll make you some food." She rose up from beside me, wiping off her tears. Mothers. They want to keep feeding you even if you're not hungry.

"You came for the wedding?" dad asked as she went into the kitchen. I nodded my head and he laid his arm around my shoulder. *"Be strong. If she's meant for you, she'll come to you eventually."*

It took them a whole day to believe that I was moving in front of their eyes. Parents' love was everlasting, I realized. It never ends no matter what.

"Do you really want to do this?" mom asked as I got dressed for Saaya'swedding. I looked at her from the mirror and,

"I don't want to hide anymore mom. I better start facing things. Running away, is only going to make me look like a coward." I said, holding her shoulders with my hands and looking into her eyes. *"Don't worry. I can take it."*

Our driver was waiting in the car at the door and I got in alone. My hands began to tremble as the car drove towards Saaya'swedding venue. I wasn't aware if my friends would be there, but I sure as hell would attend it. I prayed that I had the strength to not to ask my driver to turn the car away. I prayed that I was strong enough to attend my ex-girlfriend's wedding. The car pulled in to a stop at the entrance through the crowd. I slowly swung the door open with fear and stepped out. People, who knew me, looked at me with awe as they noticed me walk in. Heads turned to notice me as if I came back from the dead. I took a short glance at Mr. Viroodh and he gestured me with his eyes that he was glad that I was there. Saaya wasn't at the Vedic yet. I sat there silently ignoring everyone and no one made a move to talk to me either. After a while, Saaya was escorted towards the Vedic and I kept staring at her with a blank expression. It came upon her as a shock, as she was seated at the Vedic and at the sight of me sitting in the front row. She stared at me for a few seconds and then turned away. She tried not to look at me and pretended that she was happy.

Mrs. Viroodh, upon noticing me, made an aggressive move towards me but Mr. Viroodh pulled her back by her arm gently. Saaya took a glimpse at her parents and lowered her head. She turned her eyes to me once in a while but ignored looking at me most of the time. I wanted to ask her to think over it one last time but I let it pass. I prayed that she would remain as she was. I didn't have the strength to accept her back. I watched her without a blink in the eye all along; all along until the third knot of marriage. I rose up from the chair taking my eyes off her and walked away calmly with a sneer on my face. I felt empowered all of a sudden. The moment she became somebody else's wife; she had disappeared from my life. She had created for herself, a world without me in it. There was no point in waiting on a spineless love. It was time I erased all the memories that pulled me deep into my past. I had lived past my indebtedness and did my time living a lonely life. I walked away with triumph. I walked away, with tranquility. For everything we do in life, at some point of time or the other, we gotta pay. And I've been paying for it since then.The driver brought around the car to me when he saw me walk out. Apparently, he was aware of the situation too. I could see it in his eyes but he didn't utter a single word like he always used to.

Mom and dad rushed to the door as they heard the honking of the car horn. *"She's married."* I said, walking inside, past them. *"I'm starting back to Delhi in few days. It's time I started taking my work seriously."*I went out for a drive the very evening, with a box full of Saaya's gifts seated in the back; the cards and letters she gave me, gifts, stuff of hers that I preserved as precious souvenirs, her pictures, everything. I drove to the outskirts of the city which lied silent as a dead tree and burnt them to ash. It was her decision to walk out of my life, and I preferred that her memories had gone too. It had to happen eventually. Now I know that not everyone can stay strong. It was like, um, a lesson once learnt. If I continue thinking about her, I'm afraid I might start hating her. She was however right in her own way and I'm glad that she found a better guy than me. Yeah it took to me a while. I've been going to Dublin's to get drunk every day. Lying in the darkness of my room with the blinds closed. Time will change things eventually.

And here I am, in the capital city of India, working my ass off." He finished.

"You didn't try and talk to her? You serious?" I chuckled at him as he stopped the car by a shop and bought a pack of cigars.

"Have you ever been in love with Tianna, Vian?" he questioned, as he paid for the cigarettes.

"Yes, and we broke up. I'm still stuck with her. I just can't get out of it." I answered, wondering why he asked me that though it was all there in the draft which he previously read.

"There are two kinds of love. One that we fight for to win it and the other we walk away from to save it. You answered my question that you're still stuck, without losing that smile on your face. Don't worry. You got out. Just as I got busy with my work to forget Saaya, you got busy with my story and forgot Tianna. If you didn't, you wouldn't be here now. You better start looking for another girl. The girl from your class whom you have a crush on, perhaps?" he chuckled. "What's that story? You haven't written about that?"

"Nah that was stupid. When I started my college, I liked a girl. She was cute. Thought I could talk to her and ask her out, but she already had a boyfriend." I told him. "But what about you? Do you have anyone running in your mind?"

"You know what? I left that task to my parents. The next girl I'm going to fall in love with, is going to be whomever my parents would want me to marry."

"You serious?"

"Yeah?"

"You want to marry a total stranger?" I asked trying to tease him.

"Yes."

"You realize that she might not be what you expect her to be, don't you?"

"I learnt how to adjust. I shall try and compromise." He cut me off.

"I'm not gonna say another word." I broke into a heavy laugh and he joined me as well. We sat there in his car, smoking and having a good laugh.

"So what's with Daphne? Anything going on between you which you didn't write about?" he joked, looking at me tauntingly.

"No, no no. I better let us remain friends. She's not into me either." I cut it off.

"Not ready to get into complications yet, huh?"

"You can say that." I chuckled. "So you're totally out of it now? And happy?" I asked.

"Yes." He snapped. "That's the important thing in life, right? To be happy?"

"Yeah." I readily agreed. "But where's the fun in that?"

#21

I spent the weekend with Tim to get to know him better. I hadn't seen the slightest sign of sadness on his face, or perhaps he had learned to hide all his pain behind a smile.Tim Koster wasindeed a guy who can surprise. Saaya's love was nothing but an emotional element that changed him into a better man.Tim Koster could have been arrogant, egoistic, spoilt brat but he was no lesser than a man who was could be hurt. He had an architect job which he took pretty seriously. He would be leaving to Mumbai soon after the end of his contract for his job. Probably he'd get married to a girl with whom he'd fall in love again, now that he had learnt the value of a loved one. Evidently, he didn't seem to be too sentimental after what he went through.

I had satisfactorilyfinished what I had started; My pursuit on Tim Koster's story, did me a lot of good. I realized, that losing hope is not an option. I realized that everything happens for a reason. But there was something else which was going wrong. I realized that there was one last thing I was destined to do. There was something which I haven't commenced yet. I booked my tickets straightaway and flew to Mumbai. I was tensed as hell to be frank as I sat in the plane, looking out the window. I wasn't sure if whatever I was going to do, would work or not. There was only one way to find out; to make a big move. I literally ran out of the airport to hire a cab and jumped in when I got one.

"Where are you?" I asked hastily, as Anil answered my call. The cab driver was looking at me through the rear view mirror expecting me to give him an address for the drop.

"Where else? As if I have a job to do. Hanging out at coffee day as usual." He joked.

"Pali Hill." I told the cab driver, holding my phone away from my ear and he turned his eyes onto the road from the rear view mirror in an impatient manner.

"Daphne is here as well." Anil continued. I heard that you were in Delhi? How's Tim?"

"He's doing great. He'll be back to Mumbai in few months."

"So are you going back to New York?" he questioned.

"No, I'm in Mumbai now. I'm looking forward to having a talk with my parents about something important. I'm coming to you now. We shall talk."

"What is it about?" he asked, curiously.

"I'm on my way. Let's talk in person."

"Sure." He agreed and dropped the call.

A sudden nervousness kicked my heart and fastened my breath. I rubbed my palms together to wipe the sweat off of them. I sat there in the cab, trying to keep my stress. It was time I broke out of the past that had kept me chained. It was time I made myself an exemption from a wretched life. The lesson from Tim's story was worth the wait and struggle. It was like the wait for an afterlife. Life could be so intimate and ugly. It's the way we treat it that makes it beautiful. I could be awfully pious towards my life. What could go wrong as long as I was determined to be happy? All anyone would remember of Tim was how crazy he was and how sensitive he could be; how loving he could be; I wished that the drive to the coffee day was longer. As I approached, I felt a cold touch of cowardice in my gut.

"Right here." I instructed the cab driver to pull the car by café coffee day. I got out nervously, paying him off and walked towards the entrance, pulling myself together. I squeezed through the door as I pulled it open and Anil came jumping onto me.

"You finally did it." He started. "And your story is now complete."

"I may have lost the deal. I did give the story a reasonable ending though."

He gave me a hug and when released, Daphne held my hand tight and stared at me with admiration. "You still found him."

"Thank you." I said, and held her with my palms, by her shoulders. I then took her hands into mine, and,

"Daphne!" I called.

"Mmhmm?"

"I may not be a great guy. I'm not so good at

surprises, and I have no idea if I'm going to do this right; but I'm definitely not the guy who sits back without making a move and lose things." She stared at me, puzzled. "I don't care what your answer is going to be. I'm just going to go for it. Will you marry me?" I slowly went down on my knee, to make it look perfect just the way Tony and Tim did, but somehow I had a feeling I looked stupid.

Daphne didn't utter a single word but continued to stare at me with a blank expression. I waited impatiently, worried, afraid, ready to be embarrassed and devastated if she had reacted otherwise. "What took you so long?" she nudged me by my head and I got me up to my feet to hug her.

"There is something about Mumbai. Anything could happen." Anil commented as he patted me. I cried out of happiness as she remained still with her arms around my neck. The tears that I had shed then were the last.

I shed a thousand tears out of sorrow that helped suppress the pain; but the tears out of extreme joy from Daphne's happiness, gave me the meaning to the agony I had been through.

Few months from then I settled in India with my parents. Mitali and Ryna bought a home a few miles away from ours. It was then the wait for Tim Koster's return. The excitement filled in, in all of them, as they awaited Tim's presence. Daphne and I would be married soon. We thought having Tim at the wedding would be so cool. If it wasn't for him, I wouldn't have found Daphne. Kosters had never been so happy. Their childish love towards their only child; As for Saaya Viroodh, she lived on the hasty decision she made. Perhaps she was adapted to the life with her husband and was happy though she loved Tim. She ended up as a complete stranger to Tim. She was happy too, accepting the reality of life; accepting a life of moving on. Saaya and Tim both realized by then, no matter how hard we try for something to happen, if it's not meant to be, it shall never be. They accepted each other's separate ways of leading their lives and lived with no regrets. Maybe that's how we love people; Love, with a hope; hope, that they should be happy with or without us.

People say that the first love is the best love and the first cut, the deepest. But heartbreak is just a vicious game thatlove plays with the mind.

ABOUT THE AUTHOR

Subhash was born on November 7, 1989, Andhra Pradesh, single child to his parents, did his schooling in St. John's Higher Secondary School, Gannavaram. Since high school, he's passionate about writing. Started off with small poems and short stories to novels. He's won many awards in drawing and paintings during school out of which 'Best child artist,' is one, and best outgoing student award for western dance. Although, drawing and dance remained hobbies, desire for writing turned into a passion. After school, he continued his education in Visakhapatnam and did Bachelors and then Masters in Business Management. He's currently working in a corporate company in Human Resources-Talent Acquisition domain. His previously published books are Book of love and emotions, and Voyage of the crystal sphere, and working on a crime and investigation novel.

www.ingramcontent.com/pod-product-compliance
Lightning Source LLC
Chambersburg PA
CBHW032005170626
46807CB00006B/2652